Final Voyage and Other Science Fiction Stories

Final Voyage and Other Science Fiction Stories

Basil Wells

Edited by Richard Simms

Richard Simms Publications

This paperback first edition published in 2016

Richard Simms Publications, Surrey, England

ISBN: 978-0-9930387-1-6

With special thanks to Morgan Wallace.

For more information please visit The Basil Wells Tribute Site:

http://basilewells.tripod.com

Contents

Introduction

Basil Wells sold his first short story, a grim science fiction tale called "Rebirth of Man," to the pulp magazine *Super Science Stories* in 1940. Although he was to write in the fields of weird fantasy, mystery and westerns down the years, science fiction remained the genre in which he was most prolific in a published career spanning five decades.

A devoted family man, born and educated in Pennsylvania with a Christian heritage, he was employed for nearly thirty years in a factory running chain machines for a company that made zippers for clothing. As a sideline to his day job, raising a family and maintaining a small farm where he lived near his birthplace of Springboro, Wells carved out a niche for himself in the wide ranging (but not always particularly lucrative) magazine short story market.

A quick look at the checklist of sources at the end of this book should indicate to the reader the number of different periodicals he was able to sell to. In the 1940s and early '50s he placed numerous stories in various pulp magazines. With the end of the pulp era (by the late 1950s they had all disappeared) his short fiction was from thereon to be found in the variety of digest-sized fiction magazines that, to some degree, carried on the tradition of the pulps.

In addition to this, Wells, being very active in the world of science fiction fandom (he was a member of several fan organisations and liked to attend conventions and socialise in the science fiction community), placed many of his short stories in fanzines. In fact, he was to contribute much of his work to amateur and semi-professional magazines until well into his retirement in the 1990s. It's worth noting here that an unfortunate result of this is that some of his finest works have not received the exposure they deserve, having appeared as they did in extremely obscure publications such as *Boojum*, *Dawn* and *Fan Warp*, titles with very low circulations that are mostly forgotten today.

So, let us move onto the rationale behind the book you are holding in your hands. A good deal of the author's early science fiction was assembled by William Crawford (a huge Wells fan and champion of his underrated writings) in the hardbound collections *Planets of Adventure* (1949) and *Doorways to Space* (1951). Interestingly, the latter title only contained stories written exclusively for that book. Two other anthologies of his science fiction and weird fantasy tales appeared in the 1970s, although these were self-published by Wells himself and limited to very small print runs.

However, a large number of tales have not been reprinted since they originally appeared in magazines. This collection gathers together eleven outstanding science fiction stories from the 1950s that have never been available before in book form.

The first story in this volume was published in the December 1950 issue of the very short-lived pulp magazine *Out of This World Adventures*. "Under Martian Sands" is a fast-paced space opera adventure with a planetary setting. The Mars Wells writes of is in the grand tradition of Edgar Rice Burroughs, who was a major influence on his early science fiction. This story also brings to mind the work of Leigh Brackett, a contemporary of Wells whose own Martian tales were written with that same sense of wonder. One can only wonder today how much the two writers swapped notes and influenced each other. The pair happened to be good friends for many years. Brackett and her husband Edmond Hamilton (another fine author) were close neighbours of Wells and his wife Margaret, living as they did just across the border in Ohio.

When the action in "Under Martian Sands" moves beneath the surface of the planet, our hero and heroine encounter a bizarre, out of time medieval milieu of castles, forests and marauding swordsmen. This is a theme the author explored throughout his career in stories such as "Power for Darm" (1949) and again, the Burroughs influence is felt.

Moreover, it should be admitted that the early imaginative literature of Wells is replete with certain fantasy elements, alongside the trappings and common motifs of science fiction used by other authors in this period. Wells was, after all, a fan of the genre and people I have spoken to who were lucky enough to have met him have commented on his modesty about his own contribution to science fiction. I would beg to differ with him on this, as his stories are very much his own; he had a highly individualistic writing style and his tales are permeated with brilliantly inventive concepts. In later years, Wells remarked that had he not been so determined to experiment and go against the advice of some of the magazine editors he sold his short fiction to, more of his stories may have seen the light of day. What inspired him to be different and explore new ideas may well have derived from his reading in the 1930s of the outré fiction of Clark Ashton Smith. Notwithstanding this, "Under Martian Sands" is typical of his dozens of planetary romance yarns from the 1940s and '50s and I am honoured to reprint it here.

"Monster No More" (1953) was published in *Orbit Science Fiction*, another magazine that only lasted for a few issues. The story takes place on the planet Ghakk, situated many light years from our solar system. A generation spaceship from Earth has crash-landed there, killing the captain and crew, with only a handful of passengers having survived by jettisoning to safety in emergency pods, their life saving capsules thus scattered across the surface of the planet, with a few others finding their way down using parachutes.

During the ship's journey of many aeons across the void of interstellar space, the occupants of the vessel had been exposed to cosmic rays, resulting in the havoc of mutated genes. Countless years later, the descendants of the original survivors of the ship's impact have splintered into different factions on the planet's surface, according to their varying physical and mental mutations. With each tribal group considering itself to be truly human, a motley trio of misfits choose to rebel, turning their backs on this prevailing culture of prejudice and setting out on an odyssey of discovery and adventure across an alien landscape in what is truly one of Wells' greatest stories. The vivid descriptions of an extraterrestrial world and the sense of growing friendship between the characters make this a joy to read. Indeed, the theme of brotherhood is a recurring one in his fiction;

an obvious reflection of his own Christian values and beliefs in family and tolerance for others.

The next story, "Ship of the Fog Seas" (1955), appeared in *Spaceway Science Fiction*, a Los Angeles based magazine edited and owned by none other than Wells aficionado William Crawford. This is one of several adventures the writer set on the imaginary, parallel world of Thrane, an alternate Earth that exists in another dimension. The plot sometimes reads like an exotic travelogue as the characters find a way to survive in an uncharted landscape. "Ship of the Fog Seas" is also noteworthy for its use of one of the author's most brilliant ideas, the super mech. By the use of a device known as a *mentrol*, humans are able to control by proxy (and see through the eyes of) synthetic humanoids known as mechs. These robots are able to withstand extreme temperatures and poisonous atmospheres, making them indispensable in exploring new and dangerous alien environments, their superhuman strength making them of additional use when it comes to hand to hand combat, as depicted in a memorable scene in this tale aboard a seafaring vessel.

The mech gimmick was one that Wells reused time and again in his science fiction. Those reading the stories I have assembled here will no doubt notice that many of them share the same hardware or concepts. Indeed, one can view much of Wells' work in this genre as taking place in the same future universe. Other recurring inventions that crop up throughout this collection are the *expoder*, a hand weapon that fires lethal darts, *iberno*, a drug that induces a cataleptic paralysis, and the *nik-nik* bush and *thidin* vines, plants native to Venus. That is, an anachronistic Venus with a breathable atmosphere and amphibian natives, as imagined by speculative fiction writers back in the day!

Now all of this is, of course, incidental detail. But it's fun to notice these things and marvel at how extensive was the author's vision of the future and space exploration. And also to wonder how, if more of his stories had been picked up by editors, Wells' work in this regard may well have gone on to reach the same exalted status of, for example, Jack Vance's Gaean Reach series.

From reading various articles about Wells, it is apparent that the extra income from sales of his work would have come in handy for a man raising a family. But he also wrote as someone who truly loved the genres of science fiction and weird fantasy and first and foremost wished to entertain his readership. In this respect he had a similar ethos to the British science fiction author E. C. Tubb; the driving impetus behind much of his fiction being a determination to write stories that other fans would enjoy.

But as I've mentioned previously, Wells was an experimentalist as well as a spinner of colourful, action packed adventure stories, revelling in the utter strangeness of many of his more bizarre contributions to the realm of fantastic literature. The following six stories in this collection were mostly sold to the magazines *Worlds of If* and *Fantastic Universe* and are fine examples of his penchant for experimentation and curious, futuristic settings. At times, one can see the more reflective side to his writing, as in the haunting, nuclear holocaust yarn "Sole Survivor" (1957) and the whimsical vignette "Memorium" (1956). The latter story is a mood piece that showcases the author's fascination for corrupted words, with names that have shortened over time as language alters through the ages; the boy who talks to the old man in this tale refers to his grandparents as "Granthr" and "Gramr."

"Stalemate" (1954), set in the near future, is unlike anything else I have read by this author and was the first of numerous works Wells contributed to *Worlds of If*. In an artificial satellite world orbiting the Earth, two soldiers battle it out to the death with basic weapons in a small scale combat arena set up by the United Nations as a means of resolving disputes between sovereign states on the planet below. An unlikely friendship forms between the adversaries, that theme of understanding and brotherhood common to so much of the author's short fiction.

The value of friendship is an important element in "The Pioneers" (1955), as is the need for the central characters to adopt a frontier style resourcefulness to survive as colonists on an alien planet. In fact, despite the otherworldly settings, so many of Wells' protagonists exhibit a practical minded competence, a survival instinct that is surely influenced, at least in part, by the author's own tough rural upbringing. Indeed, he once wrote of the important life lessons he learned from his parents and the influence they had on his life. Overcoming the odds, a never-say-die attitude and a sense of family are attitudes and beliefs that are reflected in his stories and "The Pioneers," a harsh, gritty and yet uplifting tale, is a fine example of this side to his writing.

The rather poignant "Moment of Truth" (1957), set on Mars, is an altogether different take on the pioneer theme and again showcases a gentler aspect to his writing, in addition to being a lesson in brevity. Wells always tended to keep his stories moving fast, with the action developing at an uncompromising pace (perhaps too rushed for some tastes), but mood pieces such as this are examples of an even more trimmed prose style.

Published in the same year, the plot of "Second Sight" takes place in a dystopian tomorrow, a vast cityscape of skyscrapers and raised, moving walkways across endless levels. A blind man acquires a new lease of life in this metropolis by use of a super mech. I cannot recall reading another of his stories quite like this one and the narrative twists and inventiveness are to be admired, although of course the super mech is an idea Wells recycled several times.

I have a special fondness for the final two stories in this book. "Utility Girl" (1959) follows the ups and downs of life aboard a trading starship for its captain and a newly employed apprentice, known as an "ute." There is a romance bubbling under the surface in this fascinating chronicle of deception and intrigue, a trait it shares with the last story collected here, "Final Voyage" (1957), which is narrated by a sentient spaceship. Just how this freighter, battered and having seen better days (the *Janelace* is a far more interesting precursor to the *Millennium Falcon*, I would say!) has achieved self awareness is never explained, and I kind of admire the cavalier, who-gives-a-damn nature of that. I believe Wells knew he had a good idea and just ran with it, and it is great that he did, as this tale has lingered in my memory many years after first reading it.

Grounded in the swamplands of Venus and with a down at heels captain and crew, the ship is prepared against the odds for an ultimate trip back into space in order to avert a war between Earth and the natives of Venus who are rebelling against their colonial masters. As ever, the plot moves along swiftly. "Final Voyage" is a marvellous example of condensed fiction and also features some humorous interchanges among the characters—Wells had a good ear for dialogue. And the subplot of a love story means this is a planetary romance in more ways than one!

Basil Wells wrote some of his very best science fiction in the 1950s and I trust these stories will illustrate that and inspire anyone new to his writings to seek out more of his work. In the preceding decade he penned many other great stories in this genre and I hope to publish a collection of some of those in the near future.

In the 1960s more superb science fiction from Wells appeared in magazines, although it is sad to note that every one of the periodicals the stories in this book are drawn from no longer exists. With so many of his markets disappearing, in later decades Wells turned increasingly to the small press and fanzines for an outlet. As I noted before in this essay, it's a shame that some of his most accomplished science fiction tales remain virtually unknown to all but a few.

Moreover, corresponding with a relative of the author some time ago, it was related to me that his family felt he and Spielberg should have met, as a good deal of Wells' science fiction would be ideal for film adaptation, especially in the light of recent advances in special effects. When one considers the out-of-body concept of his super mechs, roaming through an alien wilderness in "Ship of the Fog Seas," it brings to mind (as Wells enthusiast Richard Lupoff pointed out recently) James Cameron's movie *Avatar*.

Wells' story was published over fifty years earlier!

Richard Simms
Surrey, England
March, 2016

Under Martian Sands

The last great empire of Mars, a series of fertile islands in the heart of a shallow marshlike sea near the equator, came abruptly to an end sometime in the Dark Ages of Earth. Less than a thousand Martian years have passed since the red sands swallowed the Sea of Raba and its several score doomed cities and towns ...

It was in the last years of the empire that science reached its peak. During the reign of Raba Dagan, the Wise, scientists shook off the shackles of gravitation and voyaged in huge metal ships to the moons, and to Venus and Earth. The trading ships of Raba exploited the savage tribes existing at either pole, and her miners reopened long-abandoned mines rimming the dead sea bottoms.

Then, with the death of Raba Dagan, came the first of a series of plundering Voldurians, better known as Toads, gray-fleshed, lumpy, four-foot entities from outer space. And almost overnight the sea of Raba vanished. The hungry red sands, unchecked now, swallowed the ravaged islands and buried the domes.

To the north and to the south fled the survivors, there to battle and mingle their blood with the dwindling savage descendants of earlier civilizations. Yet the memory of their vanished fertile homeland persisted in their legends and was woven into the intricate structure of their theism.

The dune-buried islands and dead cities became a lost paradise that was to be eventually restored to its pristine culture and fertility ...

From "Ancient Cultures of Mars"
by Redford Blys, published by
Red Planet Pubs., Inc., 2041 A.D.

Jud Lee ran stubby brown fingers through his snowy hair before he let the pressure helmet drop back in place. Despite the laboring pressure pumps the air in the leaky cabin of the prospecting helicopter was uncomfortably thin. For the last three days he had lived, eaten, and slept almost exclusively in his pressure suit.

"Lopez!" he called as he snapped on the ship-to-ship audiophone.

The receivers in his helmet rattled in response. Have to check for loose connections or use the spare helmet, he decided. He bumped the transparent faceplate with a hooded wrist and the voice cleared.

"… speaking."

"Almost in the heart of Raba Depression," he said, his eyes continuing their endless sweep of the desolate dunes and ridged hollows. "No sign of water or desert growth. Two ruined cities off to the north. One just ahead."

"No luck here either." Vincent Lopez's voice was unsteady. "We have but a week remaining, my friend."

"If we could only blast the Toads out of the northern canals, we'd have water in plenty. Ten cruisers from Earth would do the trick. But we do nothing. Let them force us off Mars or use all our profits buying water!"

"Si," agreed Lopez bitterly, "but the Rhett Peace Pact says no. For no longer raiding Venus and Earth, we give the northland of Mars to the invaders."

"South Mars Limited maybe had a finger in the pie. Their polar waterways are free of grafting Voldurians."

Lopez grunted assent. "Reminds me—seen anything of that SML passenger liner reported missing yesterday?"

"Nope. Uh, wait a minute. Something down here. Outcrop of rock maybe, or a building …

"Dropping down to a hundred feet … Uh, oh! It's the ship all right. Half buried in a dune and shattered. Must have exploded."

"What's your position, Jud?"

Lee snapped back the readings, easing the heli down toward the base of the marching dune.

"Stepping out to look her over, Lopez. Stand by."

"Heading for you. Visibility almost zero. Sandstorm kicking up." Lopez snapped out something in disgusted Spanish.

"Not bad here. Better climb above it. So long."

Lee took his featherweight sand spade and left the heli's cabin on the side opposite the stiff southern breeze. He swung to the left, around the swirling turtle-paced toe of the marching hillock of ruddy sand.

Here it was more sheltered and in a dozen paces he had reached the twisted debris of the half-covered wreck.

He cleared away the sand swiftly. In two minutes he had wriggled through the burst-open cabin's wall. He gulped at what he saw.

A minute later he was calling Lopez. "Five passengers and three crew members. All dead."

"Emergency call made it six passengers, one female."

"All men." Lee frowned at the slowly advancing wall of sand particles. The breeze was growing in power. "She may have been thrown free. Cabin split open like a nut."

"We'll radio from the base." Lopez's voice was strained. "Getting really knotty here, Jud. Better take off before it gets you."

The transmitter of the little Mexican partner of Jud Lee clicked off. The water prospectors and mineralogists of Northern Mars Incorporated always worked in pairs. And never at greater distances than forty miles from one another. So the desert storm would soon be upon Lee.

He took off, the sudden blast of thin air as he topped the dunes almost smashing him downward again. He climbed as fast as the sky prop's blades permitted. And his hands froze on the controls.

A pinpoint of light blossomed in the growing dusk of swirling dust clouds and endured for brief seconds—an emergency flare. Less than a quarter mile to the north it was. He headed toward it and finally spotted a pressure-suited shape kneeling in the shelter of a minor dune.

Somehow he landed less than a dozen feet beyond the woman. She came crawling through the blast of the sky prop and he yanked her into the cabin. He sent the ship lurching skyward, and, once clear of the sand, locked its controls for 500 feet.

The helmet slid from the woman's dusty head. He saw a tear-stained face and long reddish-brown hair. Her eyes were big, blue and staring with the terror she had known. Lee took in the flabby cheeks and the pouting lips and did not like what he saw.

"I'm thirsty," she said. "Give me some water."

Lee held a water flask for her and pushed her hands away after the first swallows. "Uh, uh," he said.

"Give me that water, Grandpa," she snarled weakly at him. "My father'll put you back at mining if you don't."

"Your father will?" Lee laughed. "And who's he?"

"Commander Banton, you fool! Now give me that drink."

Lee stuffed the flask into his pressure suit's zippered belly pouch. He snapped on the transmitter, calling Lopez again. Between calls for his comrade he studied his unwelcome passenger.

"So you're 'Louse' Banton," he mused. "Worst spoiled brat on Mars. And from South Mars, too!"

"My name is Lois!" the girl fairly screamed. "And I am not a brat!"

"Shut up," ordered Lee abruptly. "Yeah, this's Lee. You okay, Lopez? Great ...

"Got the girl. Jet-happy little dame left the wreck and started off on foot! Honest ... Banton's daughter ..."

Lois slapped at Lee's tough pressure mask and he held her off with one hand, grinning sourly at her gasping rage.

"Meet you at base," he concluded, "in an hour or so."

Half an hour later he was not so sure he'd make the base. He was making no headway against the raging torrent of sand-laden atmosphere; in fact he guessed he was losing the battle, and the battered heli's cabin was slowly wrenching apart at its welded seams.

Once he'd climbed to four thousand feet, to find the wind yet more turbulent there. Cross currents of air had tossed the little mapping ship about and forced him groundward. And the power of the hurricane had kept growing.

Both he and the Banton girl were strapped into their seats as the heli slammed about crazily. Abruptly the controls went lifeless in his hands. Something had given way. Helplessly, they were carried before the storm. The instruments were crazy, here in the Raba Depression they were far below the arbitrary sea level as it was, and now they could not be read correctly.

"May crash any minute, Lopez!" Lee shouted through his throat mike.

Uselessly, Lopez's faint voice was requesting his position, but before Lee could answer, the crash came. A freakish swirl of the sand-laden air slowed the ship momentarily, and it dropped like a rock. There was a brutal snapping impact, and then a blackness the storm could not equal.

After a time Lee was conscious of the cutting blast of air that probed through a great split in the top of the cabin. Only now the roof was in front of him. There was the taste of salty blood in his mouth. And he was no longer strapped in the control chair.

Clumsily he groped to the locker where the protective sand masks were stored and took out two of them. One he slipped over his pressure helmet and the other he took to the girl's sprawled body.

"Keep your filthy paws off me," she snarled savagely. His audiophones rattled. Her breath gurgled unevenly.

She clawed at his hands, but he persisted in his task of strapping on the mask, and an extra belt of water flasks and oxygen cylinders. She was only semi-conscious, and he was forced to carry her toward the gaping rent. Only then did complete understanding return to her.

"What—where are we going?" she demanded pettishly.

"Have to start off on foot, look for a deserted city or other shelter."

Lois Banton laughed nastily. "Hah! You jeered at my ignorance in leaving the wrecked flyer. And now you do the same."

Lee shrugged. "Sure. *You* crashed in comparatively decent weather. The wreckage remained exposed. But in five minutes, ten feet of sand may bury the heli. The dunes build swiftly in such a hurricane."

The girl gazed fearfully at the rising level of sifting sand over what had been the control panels. She fairly flung herself at the opening. Lee caught her sand boots just in time and pulled her back. Calmly he snapped a ringed ten-foot line of tough nylon into her belt and into his own. Then he checked his sand spade, pouched solar torch, and pressure-proof zippered holster where his compact machine-gun lay.

"We could anchor ourselves to the ship by a hundred-foot line," he told her calmly as he set the transmitter for thirty-second intervals of automatic signals, "but we'd soon be buried too. Only chance is drifting before the wind."

Lois' eyes were streaming tears.

"But there's no water out there," she quavered, "and our oxygen will run out."

"Then we'll use the hand pumps on our suits." Lee was angry, suddenly. "As for water there is little loss, perhaps a pint escapes in a day from these outfits."

He pushed her out the opening and followed swiftly, the blast of the storm hurrying them along. He caught a glimpse of the heli and a building ridge of red dust behind it.

They stumbled through a ruddy darkness that rustled and chewed at their tough pressure envelopes. They leaned back against the wind, their sand boots slogging mechanically along. The surge of the storm currents threatened to send them hurtling skyward, chiplike. Even the shifting ridges of the dunes offered little protection, and a moment's halt buried them to the knees.

The curved solidity of a wall jarred Lee back into realization of his surroundings. Time had lost all meaning and weariness had dulled his senses. He was astonished to discover Lois yet on her feet, her body flattened against the obstruction.

"Domed city!" he croaked, his throat thick.

The girl's teeth showed whitely through the begrimed faceplates of her sand mask and helmet. She was trying to speak but he heard nothing, the communication cables linking them had broken or his audiophone receiver had finally quit.

He inched along the slow curve of the vast dome toward the left, and perhaps a hundred feet further on found a ragged crevice in the semi-opaque shell roofing the dead city's dust-choked ruins. He squeezed through to a catwalk of spidery looking, but enduring, metal, and drew Lois in beside him.

Only five feet below them, the highest of the ancient towers and flat-roofed dwellings sprouted from the sand. Lee knew that their bases might be a hundred feet further down, perhaps more. Eventually the outer level of sand and the inner level would coincide. That this dome must have been less badly shattered by the raiding invaders of a thousand years before, he could well believe. Most of the dead towns were completely buried.

They moved to the right until the spurting spray of sand through the wide slit in the dome could no longer reach them. Lee discovered the phone cable was unlinked and reclipped the contacts.

"I'm going outside again," he told the girl, taking out his solar torch, "to mark our entrance. Then we'll hunt for shelter in the ruins."

He lengthened the nylon cord with another ten-foot length, before battling outward again, and then, above his head, he burned a sooty broad arrow into the dome's crystalline surface. To the left of this he burned: LEE, in two-foot letters. And on the opposite side of the crevice he put another, longer, arrow.

This done he reentered the huge dome and lay, exhausted, upon the hard metallic ribs of the catwalk. Lois was sprawled there too, mouth slack, sleeping. The effort to stand again was too great. He closed his eyes.

Lee was smothering, his lungs gasping for air. He struggled to an elbow and opened his eyes to a dust-swirling twilight. The storm had not eased while he slept.

The oxygen cylinder was exhausted. Stale air sickened him, and his temples were throbbing as he switched over to the spare tank. When that was gone they'd have to rely on the emergency hand pumps to fill them again with compressed air.

He breathed deeply and switched on the girl's extra tank. She stirred and sat up too. He grinned wryly at her contorted features.

"Hard bed," he said. "Even sand is better."

Lois squirmed uncomfortably, stretching her cramped legs and arms. She stood up, looking out over the mile-wide extent of the dome's foggy disc. "Now what?" She yawned. "Any chance of rescue soon?"

Lee shook his head. "Not until the storm's over. May be a day, may be a week. Our exit's blown shut too, I see."

The crevice by which they had entered was sealed again, and a rounded ramp of sand led down to the dome's uneven floor. Lee led the way to this and slid and stumbled down it, the girl trailing.

"Might as well hole up in the ruins," he advised. "Maybe we can seal out some of the dust so our hand pumps will not clog so fast."

Lois did not reply. She had withdrawn an arm from her suit's inflated right sleeve and was munching at an oval bar that looked like candy. Lee jerked at her other arm, making her drop the remaining fragment.

"That's emergency ration," he said sternly, "food for a week. You're going to be sorry."

"Yah!" spat out the girl, grimacing angrily at him.

Suddenly she doubled over, her face paling and yellowing to a hideous green hue. For several minutes she was violently sick, the cramped confines of her helmet and pressure suit but multiplying the discomforts of a cramping disgorging stomach.

After a time she was better, and Lee smothered a smile as she glared at him. He headed again toward the oval doorway of a rounded tower of seamless yellowed plastic, the same material of which the enormously thick skin of the dome was constructed.

Inside, a vast, high-ceilinged chamber opened. And here the light seemed to have brightened, perhaps because the dust cloud was thinned. Lee uncapped his solar torch, cutting its radiance to less than normal noontime illumination.

Vast murals, their colors bright and fresh and the glistening protective coating of diamond-hard transparency unmarred by the centuries, covered the inner walls. Lee blinked his eyes, startled, as he saw familiar animals and vegetation, not of Mars, but of Earth! And then he recalled the legends of the savage natives of the polar waterways, stories of great ships crossing to Earth and Venus.

One wall depicted scenes of Earth; jungles, seas, and cultivated countrysides with hilltop castles and thatched huts of stone. One figure was that of a mail-clad warrior astride a masked and hooded horse. Here was proof that Martians had visited Earth during the Middle Ages, this and the relief maps just below the murals.

The other wall represented scenes on Venus, recognizable to Lee, although he had never been there. Froglike natives, *Butrads*, he saw, and the ever-present aquatic growth of *thidin* vines. The paintings were as lifelike and colorful as three-dimensional photographs.

"This must have been old Raba Dagan's headquarters, Lois," he said, turning to the pale-faced girl.

They were now near the further end of the lofty hall, where twin oval ports stood invitingly open. The right hand door opened into a smaller room, its walls also decorated with pictures. Lois stepped inside and Lee followed.

Sudden emptiness opened in the pit of Lee's stomach; it was like a long-continued drop into a mineshaft. The oval opening into the outer chamber gave way to a blurring succession of rock strata and black galleries.

Lois so far forgot her dislike for Lee that she clung to his arm in terror. "We're falling!" she screamed. "Stop us! Stop us!"

"Don't worry," he told her, "this is probably an automatic elevator of some sort."

As though to confirm his words the "room" slowed and stopped opposite another oval doorway. They stepped out into a dreary cavern of a room that was lightless save for Lee's solar torch. For another ten seconds or so the platform remained opposite and then it sank away smoothly into the depths.

Only a faintly luminous mistiness, smokily brown and falling steadily, was to be seen in the square shaft.

"Now what, vac brain?" demanded the girl. "We're stuck here maybe a mile below the surface."

"The other shaft should have a current of this same inert gas rising upward," Lee suggested. "Let's see."

They took the four steps necessary to reach the other opening, looking down into a vacancy like that they had just quitted. Lois laughed jeeringly. Apparently her stomach was returning to normal, and she was again her usual disagreeable self.

"Disappointed, Grandpa?" she asked.

Lois was possibly nineteen or twenty and Lee was twenty-five. It was his prematurely snow-white hair that earned this nickname, a freakish result of a glancing bullet in one of the unending affrays between miners of SML and his own company. He grinned. After all he'd called her Louse, first.

"Nup. Be another platform along soon."

A minute passed. Lois sniffed triumphantly. And then a bulky something came sliding softly up from below and came to rest in the shaft. Its oblong entrance almost exactly matched that of the mysterious barren chamber.

"Going up, Miss Banton?" asked Lee. "No charge."

Lois shook her head violently. "No! Let's keep going down and see what's there. We might find a treasure or mines."

There was new respect in Lee's voice as he agreed. It took a certain amount of courage, or bravado, to go downward into the unknown when a way to the surface was waiting. Despite her words her voice had quavered a trifle at the end.

A moment later they were aboard a platform in the other shaft and dropping steadily downward.

The platform cage glided to a stop again, its seventh, and a well-lighted corridor lay beyond the oval port. Lois went swiftly out of the unmoving compartment with Lee at her side. And for the first time he noticed how their pressure suits wrinkled and flapped about their bodies.

He tested the outer pressure by cracking the helmet valve. There was no escape of oxygen. Gingerly he sniffed, sniffed again more deeply—and tugged at his helmet until it loosened and hung back on his shoulder hinges.

"Clean air," he cried. "Air with the smell of flowers and green growing things in it! Moist air!"

Lois followed suit. For several long sobbing breaths they were content to stand there and suck in the heady fragrance of the thick air. It made them dizzy after a time, forcing them to breathe more shallowly as they peeled off their cumbersome pressure gear.

"How deep would we be," demanded Lois, "before air pressure equaled Earth Normal?"

"Plenty deep, Lois. And the air is moist!"

"So what? Our domes in South Mars are the same."

Lee muttered something uncomplimentary about "Toad Lovers" and started down the corridor. For several hundred feet it extended straight as an arrow, a softly glowing tube of perhaps twenty feet in diameter. The girl hurried after Lee.

Their now useless pressure suits and helmets, as well as the useless sand gear, they left behind. Finally Lee spoke:

"Moisture means water, possibly an underground lake or sea. North Mars Incorporated wouldn't have to close its mines. We've been in the red for the past two years buying all our water from the Toads!"

"I'm glad they're not in our hemisphere," agreed Lois.

"Yeah." Cynicism dripped from the word. His lips uncurled. "Sorry. Forget you're just a brat. Shouldn't be taking out my dislike for SML on you."

"I'm nineteen," the girl cried, "and no brat! But most of us do feel sorry for your people in the north—the women and children, that is."

"Thought you'd qualify it."

Suddenly Lee halted and his right hand went down to the gas-powered pocket gun holstered at his hip. It contained a clip of a thousand biaton-tipped needles—each needle an explosive miniature grenade. Because these were expelled, rather than fired, the common term of *expoder* was given them.

A forty-foot section of corridor had lost its glowing coating, it lay jumbled and dull on the floor, and the slimy darkness of water puddled there as well. On the left a branching corridor, also in darkness, opened. And there Lee thought he had detected movement.

His hand fell away. He laughed at himself. How could there be life here in this long-deserted necropolis? Of course the weird elevator shafts yet functioned and there was the mysterious light, but in other abandoned cities Earthmen had discovered atom-powered machines purring untended after thousands of years. At Port Bemis, his homedome, all the power they needed for lights and heat came from a single Martian power plant.

Carefully he picked his way over the debris by the dim light from beyond. He passed the intersecting emptiness, a smaller unlighted way, and then a scrabbling sound came to him. Probably Lois. He started to turn.

"Jud, behind you!" the girl's voice screamed.

His leisurely movements changed. He flung himself forward and spun about, dropping to his knees with the expoder jutting from his fist. He saw three dwarfish squatty shapes, heavy clubs upraised, almost upon him. They must have come from the unlighted passage.

And then the hand gun sewed its needles across their torsos, those missing the targets exploding against the corridor's wall. A miniature series of thunderclaps boomed along the way. But even as the echoes died away the last of his attackers fell.

Lee came forward warily, his solar torch at plus sunlight searching into the other tunnel for other foes. It was empty to a depth of perhaps a hundred feet, but it curved to the right and therefore he could see no further.

He turned again to the fallen men, discovering them to be dwarfed humanoid creatures, thick-shouldered and hairy, their teeth yellowed fangs, and with foreheads little higher than their bulging frontal sinuses. Two of the naked beast-men were dark-haired, and the other covered with matted, straw-colored hair. Yet among the native Martians of the polar regions, black hair was almost unknown; reddish-blond hair, coarse and thick as fur, being their natural covering.

And the size of their chests, when compared with the vast lung cavities of the polar natives, was pitifully inadequate. They were warped, bow-legged, and gnarled, with the filthy skin under their coarse-haired covering whiter than that of Lois.

He returned to the girl.

"Better go back, hadn't we?" he asked.

She bit her sagging lip and her damp eyes grew hot. Her body straightened defiantly. Stooping over a dead savage she found his club, a knotted cudgel longer than a man's forearm, and lifted it. She moved past Lee. "Come on, Grandpa," she challenged, leading the way.

Lee moved up beside her, his hand gun in his fingers, and his eyes alert. Together they strode down the seemingly unending length of the huge tube. Foolhardy it was, perhaps, but the water-hunger that only a native-born Martian knows, burned hot in both their hearts.

Something of the man's excitement and flaming hope had touched the girl. In her eyes was the same overpowering lust for water, and more water, that rivaled mankind's earlier madness for gold.

Less than half a mile the gallery extended into the misty glow of its inner walls. Then they came out on a wide ledge of stone, its outer wall of living granite waist-high, and realized that they perched near the roof of a vast subterranean abyss. On either side the ledge extended unbroken, an observation platform for the long-vanished citizens of the Raba Depression.

"This must have been a zoological garden, a living museum of Earth," whispered Lois softly.

The cavern floor, a thousand feet below, was almost five miles in length and half as wide. And three-fourths of its area was island-rimmed water!

Directly beneath them a grassy miniature tableland sprouted oddly familiar structures of stone—castles and crazily constructed little huddles of thatched huts. The castles, four in all, were in ruins, but about the last of them to the right, two-legged figures were moving. There, too, were a few patches of tilled ground with rowed dottings of cultivated green.

And rimming the lake, basking in the all-pervading glow of light similar to that of the corridor, lifted a mighty tangled forest of familiar, and unfamiliar, trees.

"Those wild men were Earthmen!" Lee moved slightly away from the girl's too-obvious nearness. "I thought their structure was decidedly unMartian, too-slight lung capacity."

"Must be old King Raba Dagan had quite a zoo." Lois lolled on the rocky parapet's flat top and studied the scene below. "Suppose there's another cave like this for Venusian fauna and stuff?"

Lee massaged a knuckle thoughtfully. He nodded. "Uh huh. Those murals, those paintings, were advertising the wonders of the strange life imprisoned here.

"This is a paradise, though. All this water. Means NMI won't have to close down after all."

Lois' laugh was nasty. "If we can get topside, yes. Don't forget the sand has covered the opening and your signal is buried. We may be trapped here forever."

"I hope not. Probably by now Lopez in starting to hunt for us. Or soon will be. And the crack in the dome may be uncovered again."

"Isn't it thrilling, though, Gramp?" giggled Lois. "We're like castaways—Adam and Eve in a garden—Harveth and Elise on Luna."

"Martian hill-dog and a desert cat in a bag more likely," said Lee dryly. "And we're not alone, either. Look, coming."

She turned to look in the direction his hand gun indicated, to the left. They saw a tall, broad-shouldered man, his thick black beard like a mane down across his hairy chest, and an ancient explosive-type rifle in his hand. His only garment was a rough, but effective, swathing of animal hide about his hips. He was less than twenty feet from them and the small black eye of the rifle was upon them.

Behind the savage-appearing creature clustered a dozen of the twisted dwarfs, more beasts than men, that they had already encountered.

For a long moment they fronted one another, unmoving, before the stranger's weapon dropped away and his beard split to reveal uneven white teeth. His voice was deep and unsteady, the words blurred by alien pronunciation.

"Good day, sirs," he said, apparently mistaking Lois' golden slacks and brown jacket for a masculine outfit.

"Greetings, Thug," chirped Lois. She grinned at Lee's warning frown. In an undertone she demanded, "Isn't that a perfectly good caveman title?"

Lee grunted something about fools and their heads ending in two separate sectors of space.

"Hello," he said quietly. "Earthman?"

"Indeed I am," said the bearded giant, advancing. "We are all Earthmen." His arm indicated the motley knot of little monsters at his heels.

"But you are more recently arrived, eh?"

The big man grimaced his understanding. "Thirty years ago my father found this horrible place. He came from the desert after his ship was crushed in landing."

Lee's eyes were shining. "The first spacers landed about then. What is your father's name?"

"Grant Ashley. He is dead now." He pulled an ancient pocket-watch of worn soft gold from a pouch beneath his great beard. "One hundred twenty days and—almost an hour from now—ago."

Lois bowed her head over it. "I see," she laughed, "how you knew thirty years have passed. You couldn't miss seeing this.

"But you don't look to be that old."

The big man's eyes were fixed on the girl. He took a step toward her, hands clawed in a horrible, hungry sort of way, and then another. A ghastly bubbling cry of misery and unbelieving joy wrung from his lips.

"A woman—an Earth woman," he mumbled. "Always they told me I must mate with the ugly little shes. But now G'Ash has a woman."

Lois backed away uncertainly, getting behind Lee. Lee grimaced with distaste, but held his ground.

"My woman," he said. "Sorry."

"Then I must fight you for her." The big savage dropped his rifle and bared his teeth. Then, in imitation of Lee, "Sorry."

Lee shook his head. "The little hes may fight so over their women. Not so real Earthmen. They let the woman choose."

The bearded man scratched his shaggy head. His beard again covered his teeth. He grunted grudging assent, but he continued to regard Lois hungrily. Lee knew the truce would not last.

"My father married a little she," he told Lee and the girl. He pointed down into the cavern valley toward the castle with the cultivated fields. "Mine," he added proudly, "you come there, please?"

"How many of the dwarf-men are there?" Lee wanted to know as they studied the valley.

G'Ash fiddled with his huge splayed fingers, his lips moving as he counted laboriously and silently.

"Maybe sixty-one, sixty-two or three, perhaps. Some have rebelled and hide in the forests or in the valley of the Frog People."

Lee nodded. "The Venusians. Where does it open off this valley?"

G'Ash indicated the dark opening at the left-hand end of the valley. "There," he said savagely. "Some day I will lead my people into it again."

"Are there other valleys, more lakes?"

The bearded man grunted. "At other end of the cavern. But all is water there, and the light is bad, almost gone. Also huge swimming things fill the water."

Lee looked at Lois, and then, meaningly, down into the cavern. She shook her head slightly. He turned to G'Ash.

"We must return to our friends," he said, extending his hand, "but we will return again soon."

The big man scowled, but he took Lee's hand. Suddenly he jerked the flyer toward him and his other fist crunched into Lee's jaw. A second blow landed on his temple and he felt his legs crumpling under him. Feebly he struggled to strike back, to reach his expoder.

He heard Lois screaming, and he saw the pipestem crooked legs of the degenerate warriors about him, with the last fading senses. Then cool stone was crushing his lips and nose and he knew no more.

He was penned in a time-weathered dungeon, light seeping through yard-thick walls of masonry, and silvering the cobwebs festooning the walls and ceilings. His bed was a heap of mildewed weeds and reeds on a low stone platform, and in the cell's center a tiny spring bubbled up. From this a tiny rill crossed the rocky floor and vanished into a gaping cavity wider than a man's skull.

Lee went to the narrow slit of the single window, standing on a heap of debris to do so. He looked out over the weedy patches of cultivated ground, and saw the willow-grown border of the lake. In the garden plots misshapen little women worked, their naked flesh a hideous, fish-belly white. And grotesque little dogs played with unsmiling tiny children upon the uncut grass between the gardens.

The inbred, simple-minded inhabitants of this hidden Eden beneath the ruddy desert, never laughed, and Lee, only once, heard their unintelligible speech raised in a broken sort of song. The proud knights and their humble serfs, brought here from Earth, had fallen far from their early estate.

Lee tested the walls, searching for loose masonry that could be removed. He tried the warped metal door, and found it to be strengthened by a second sturdy gate of interlocked logs and branches. Last of all he examined the ceiling, a dozen feet overhead, and found it had suffered least of all in the passing years.

His only hope of escape seemed to be through the opening cut into the walls by the spring's overflow, and toward this he started to move.

But a sound of shuffling feet in the corridor beyond arrested his steps and he faced the doorway. The overlooked clip of needles was worthless as a weapon.

G'Ash stood in the doorway, a fire-blackened lump of flesh, its white-jointed bone protruding, in his left hand. In his other fist was Lee's needle-expelling hand gun. He tossed the hunk of meat at Lee.

"Your woman fled from me," he complained, his forehead wrinkled. "She hides in the forest beside the lake with the rebellious people."

"Good for her," said Lee. "I told you we Earthlings allow the women to choose."

"You must summon her," ordered G'Ash. "Then when she is close I can capture her."

"Go in a vacuum," Lee told him. He gnawed at a huge mouthful of the underdone meat.

"You refuse?" G'Ash took a threatening step forward.

Lee gave the bone and most of the meat back to the bearded giant— in the teeth! He followed the hurled missile with his fists and the weight of his tough sand boots. But the big man weathered the storm easily. One big hand seized Lee and hurled him, stunned, against the further wall of the dungeon.

He paused only to pick up the misused joint of meat.

"When you grow hungry," he roared, "you will be glad to call your woman for me."

Lee felt the numbness leaving his battered flesh. He made no sign he knew G'Ash was about. Instead he began masticating the mouthful of meat he had retained.

The bearded savage growled and lunged off along the corridor beyond. And as his footsteps grew inaudible Lee came to his hands and knees and crawled over to the spring to drink. Then, despite the pain that every movement brought, he lowered himself into the water-slimed cavity where the little rill disappeared.

His feet found a footing on a narrow ledge; then his elbows locked him in the narrowness of the crooked channel as he slowly descended. Once he stuck fast and for perhaps twenty minutes hung there with the falling water saturating and chilling his coveralls and the garments beneath.

Then cloth ripped along his back and he was precipitated suddenly downward about eight feet into a thigh-deep pool with a slimy mud bottom. He groped about in the icy depths, his solar torch gone along with his hand gun, and came up a gradual slope of possibly twenty feet in all, to a waterless expanse of rock.

The echoes, hollow and booming, of his boots on the rocky floor, informed him that he was inside a lower cavity of considerable area. He groped along the edge of the pool, found where it overflowed, and followed the escaping thread of water.

He squeezed through narrow slits in the rocky walls and traversed vast chambers where a faint rippling play of electricity revealed inky pools and lakes. He heard splashings that only living things could make, and he armed himself as best he could with a keen-edged splinter of rock twice as large as his palm. In the depths, darting trails of pale light marked the passage of the watery denizens.

Three times he slept, his cramped limbs and aching muscles awakening him before he was rested. He was hungry, his stomach crying out for the food that successfully evaded his attempts to scoop it from the growing bitterness of the cavern pools.

Then came the moment when he wriggled upward through a narrowing slot of dank rock above the gurgling rush of piled-up water. And saw light ahead!

Once beyond the narrowing of the walls he hobbled along a widening ledge for a hundred yards—and emerged through a trailing curtain of Venusian thidin vines, and lacy, crimson-hued swamp air, into a watery valley yet larger than that of the Earthmen.

Floating islands of thidin dotted the foggy surface of the steaming lake, and along the narrow shoreline the fruit-heavy bushes of the *nik-nik* clustered. Their orange-hued husks were specked scarlet.

Lee ate the ripe fruit, the faded globes of brown with the enlarged splotches of red, as slowly as his hunger permitted. Nor did he have his fill of the crisp salmon-hued pulp and its thumb-sized black seeds when he reluctantly pushed off into the pale jungle.

He slept once before he discovered the linking passageway with the Earth cavern. It was near the mile-high arch of the cavern's roof and led upward. A well-worn trail had grooved the stubborn surface of rock to a depth of an inch.

In the Venusian cavern he had only once seen a noseless, gray-hued Frog. And that lop-eared aborigine had been paddling a living raft of thidin out in the lake. Of the Earthmen reputed to have taken refuge in the lower valley he saw not a sign.

He emerged, hours later, into a tree-roofed tunnel piercing the forest. He had taken but a dozen steps along this narrow way, when a tangle of vines and braided ropes of hide and grass, fell about him.

He struggled despairingly, his keen-edged stone slashing madly. Yet for every strand he severed, two or three more nooses fell about him. At last he lay helpless.

Three of the crooked beast-men of the lost cavern gathered about him, prancing proudly, and thumbing the points of their rusty dagger-like knives suggestively. And then a pleased gurgle of laughter made him turn his head in the other direction.

Lois Banton bent over him and began loosing the cocoon of ropes. She had changed greatly in the short time they had been apart, and Lee wondered if perhaps more than four or five days by Martian reckoning, had passed. For under her flapping ragged garments the muscles moved lithely, and the superfluous flesh had melted from her face.

"Have you loose in a minute," she said. "O'Lar, you and K'Ton help me. B'Ron can keep watch."

"Glad you're still free," grunted Lee. And was amazed to discover that he really meant it.

"We've been trying to locate you," said Lois. "But this eternal dayshine is bad. Only at the sleeping hour did we dare venture from the forests."

The last of the ropes fell away and Lee stood up. He saw now that Lois had an ancient-looking, cross-hilted sword in a clumsy scabbard of dried black leather, and that two of the squatty, club-armed hunters wore floppy sleeveless jerkins of battered chain mail.

"Found the armory of one castle," explained Lois, noting his curious gaze. "Never did get to rescue you, though. Our friend with the beard kept a guard posted." She cocked an eyebrow. "How'd you do it?"

Lee explained his escape.

She nodded. "I've been in the other cavern once. Frogs aren't friendly anymore since O'Lar"—she indicated the largest of the three renegade dwarfs—"refused to let them eat his woman."

"They understand English then and speak it!"

Lois grinned in a superior fashion. "Naturally. Ashley tried to teach them modern English among other things. He was horribly crippled, often lay helpless for weeks. Result of spacer's crash. So his brief attempts at schooling them accomplished little."

Lee dug into his inner pockets, his hand emerging at last with the useless clip of biaton needles for his captured hand gun. He showed them to the girl.

"If you'll let me have that dagger," he said, pointing to the blade she carried thrust through her sword-belt, "I'll try manufacturing a bomb."

Lois handed it over reluctantly. "Needles are dangerous to tinker with, aren't they?" she demanded.

"Uh huh. But we can't cut our way through to the dome-lifts with just clubs and a sword. Not against an expoder and a high-powered rifle."

Lee seated himself beside the trail, and, motioning the others away, set to work on the delicate task of exposing the metal-encased pinpoint of explosive biaton at the tip of three needles. In his hand gun the razor-edged trimmer key armed the needles only as they were expelled, to explode upon contact with anything more substantial than air. But this way he was holding in his hands a death more susceptible than nitroglycerin to sudden jolts.

With sticky gum from a bruised tree he gingerly sealed all the needles into their clip, leaving the three armed needles projecting further. Then he looped a slender strip of hide about the deadly thing and ran the thong up and over a low limb, securing the other end with a loosely driven peg.

Directly beneath the clip of explosive needles lay a barely exposed reef of greenish-gray rock where only lichens and moss could root.

Last of all he knotted another thin strand of hide about the peg and ran it, knee-high, across the trail where he quickly and properly secured it to another limb.

His death trap, clumsy though it was, was complete. Now he must lure the childish bearded giant into it.

Even as he plotted the man's destruction he could not but feel pity for the poor brute. Had the man been unarmed or alone he would have risked capturing him with snares, or even attempted to escape from the cavern without further conflict.

But he could take no chances on the bearded giant recapturing or killing them. News of this plentiful supply of the fluid life-blood of Mars must be carried outside whatever the cost.

G'Ash must die.

Lee started down the trail toward the castles and then retraced his steps. He tore the cord from the limb and knotted other lengths to it. The blank-faced beast-men and the girl regarded him curiously.

At a distance of a hundred yards, well inside the tunnel toward the Venusian cavern, he posted Lois with the looped end of the cord in her grip.

"We must be sure it is their leader," he said. "A wandering animal or dwarf might set off the bomb. Can you do it?"

The girl's lips tightened, but her grave eyes were steady on Lee's.

"Certainly," she said simply.

Twice Jud Lee showed himself briefly, he could not be too obvious, before G'Ash and ten of his brute-men came charging out of the ruined castle after him.

At first he ran easily, allowing G'Ash to gain on him, and then he was sprinting desperately to keep safely in advance. The prodigious bounds of G'Ash put him far in advance of his hairy followers.

He passed the ledge of exposed stone but a dozen paces in advance of the bearded savage, a lead that was swiftly being whittled down, and then flung himself to the left behind a sheltering inky black boulder.

There was a terrible explosion.

He stood up at last, ears ringing, and looked back toward the shallow pit in the trail. He saw G'Ash weaponless and broken, his eyes and forehead a bloody mass of ripped flesh, crawling sightlessly toward him!

Lois had given the rope too late a tug, probably waiting for him to reach shelter, and G'Ash was beyond its full fury.

He ran around the blinded man to where the satiny metal of his hand gun shone and sent a burst of explosive needles over the cowering heads of the hairy men. They broke before this new menace, and raced back along the way they had come.

Then he turned back toward the crawling bloody mass of flesh that was G'Ash, reluctant to destroy him, yet knowing that the man was better dead. In all the Earth cavern only G'Ash might lead an attack against them.

But the bearded savage had disappeared. Nor did a half hour of searching uncover his trail.

"I'm glad he escaped," said Lois, as they climbed the winding ramps to the upper gallery and the lifts. "We have the guns now. In a few minutes we'll be in the dome."

"I feel the same," admitted Lee. "He couldn't stop us now."

They hurried along the shining corridor, the three rebellious beast-men accompanying them, and Lee had time to consider the future. The storm would be long over now. He could tunnel out through the sand and burn outsized symbols on the dome. Then they could return to the depths until help arrived.

They passed the unlighted strip of tunnel, where the clean-stripped bones of the two beast men lay, and came to the lift.

Lee halted, his throat constricting, and the girl squeezed his arm sympathetically.

The huddle of equipment, pressure suits, helmets, sand spade, and spare belts, was gone! The dusty floor of the passage was empty. Where it had lain, the imprint of splayed naked feet was yet visible. G'Ash and his warriors had carried them off and they might never be found again.

In fact, the curiosity of G'Ash might impel him to tear the suits and pumps apart, to ruin them hopelessly.

He looked at Lois, and her eyes were steady and calm. Like him she must have been digesting the knowledge that they were trapped here now for a long time. For he doubted his ability to contrive a workable pressure suit and pumps out of the crude materials at hand.

The thought of enduring her constant companionship was not unpleasant, now that privation and danger had revealed the real character that years of self-indulgence had failed to destroy. They'd quarrel, and she would insult him and bully him unmercifully at times, he knew.

She must have sensed what he was thinking. Wordlessly she came closer and lifted her face toward his.

"Break it up," a muffled voice sounded behind them. They turned.

"Lopez!" cried Lee. "How'd you find us?"

Lopez finished removing his helmet, revealing a trim moustache and handsome features. His smile was dazzling and all for the girl.

"This fortune-hunter making trouble?" he inquired maliciously.

Lee shook his partner's shoulders. "How?" he demanded.

Lopez waved an airy hand. "That? Nothing! Plotted direction of storm's path and your last position. Discovered dome, explored same, and here I am."

He turned again to the amused girl.

"Now," he said warmly, "you are safe at last, Miss Banton. I, Vincent Lopez, will see that no harm befalls you. There is nothing to fear ..."

"Except you," supplied Lee, grinning. "Come along, Lois. Let's show our friend what paradise looks like."

Lois came to him, her eyes smiling, and they led the way again to the stone balcony overlooking the valley.

Monster No More

The Starship was in trouble. She was the first ship to span the void between solar systems. The voyage had lasted for hundreds of years, and the crew, and their grandparents, and their grandparents, had never set foot on a planet's soil.

But the years had taken their toll. The shielding of the hull was imperfect. The jets cracked and their liners could not be replaced. The air conditioning broke down constantly and there was a constant seepage of precious oxygen into outer space.

For every normal birth among the thousand crew members there were five or six mutant young. The cosmic rays, filtering through the imperfect shielding, were playing havoc. And the cereals and root crops, too, in the agricultural levels, were changing. Edible food was less plentiful. Sickness and vitamin deficiencies were wreaking havoc, as well.

Into the thin atmosphere of Ghakk, second of the three planets circling Rhebus IX, they drove the ship, braking as they swung in a tightening orbit about that desert world.

The jets crumbled swiftly and there was a flareback to the belly fuel tanks. The Starship plunged, in a long curving dive, down toward the ragged canyons and gray-dusted barrens of Ghakk.

The two escape craft still in commission quitted the stricken ship and dropped planetward on cushioning gouts of flame. And after them space-suited crewmen sprang into space and shook out their nested parachute vanes.

Only the commander and two of his faithful officers remained aboard to attempt a hopeless grounding on Ghakk.

The curving globe slid away beneath them, hiding the ship forever from the escaping crew members. And the arid deserts and wind-eroded hills came up to meet the dying ship's frosted plates.

Almost they completed the circuit of Ghakk.

A hundred miles west of the canyons where most of the crew had landed the great ship plowed into the desert, jounced high into the air, and struck again. The three officers died with the first impact.

For eighty miles the mile-long cylinder, battered and gaping at a thousand rents, skittered along—to come to rest at last in the shadowy depths of a sunken lake.

So the years passed on Ghakk, and the mutant crew members banded together, like to like, in widely separate valleys. After a time the mutants bred true—true to their own warped species—and memories of the distant system they had never seen were forgotten, quasi-religious fantasies.

And, with the centuries, the broad lake where the Starship lay submerged grew shallow and choked with the fine gray dust of Ghakk. In time, like a stranded whale she lay exposed.

The long-legged monster turned his back on the familiar green canyon depths, far below now in the great valley's shadows. He knew that he had seen for the last time the canyon of his people, and the barren little side-canyon where his parents, who had loved him in spite of his outlandish legs, had kept him hidden until he was grown.

He hoped they would not be punished too severely for their refusal to destroy him at birth. One of the Cru having discovered his refuge while hunting *pelfs*, warriors of the Cru would by now be hot on his trail.

"Let no monster live in the Valley of Cru." That was the grim law of the legless "men" of the canyon. And already a miniature blot of moving dust lay far below in the depths.

For an hour or more he trotted steadily westward through the broken splinters of dead rocky ridges and across narrow arid flats of fine-ground grayish dust. He twisted and weaved in and out, the better to confuse his trail, and where he could his rough leather sandals traversed trackless bare rock.

He passed greasy-leaved clumps of bluish growth. Pale yellowish cactii thrust grotesquely from the sun-seared soil. And the dust-smothered, toppled wall of some long-forgotten Ghakkan building reared unexpectedly in his path at intervals.

Now the native lizard race of Ghakk, which had built these buildings, was grown weak and degenerate, and the Cru had taken over their choicest canyon. Or so the boasting tales of the Cru ancients would have it. The lizard people's cities and roads were swallowed by the encroaching desert, and their ancient culture was passing with the dwindling water supply …

Something moved in a waist-high thicket close by. He drew his only hand weapon, a long, chip-sharpened dagger of red igneous stone, and he freed the stout, short bow across his shoulder the more easily to reach it.

The clump of brush was less than five feet in width. He stooped, scooped up a handful of the gritty dust, and flung it into the growth.

The flesh of a hairy pelf would be good … if this was a pelf. Alert and ready, he sheathed his knife even as his bowstring snapped into its nock.

A coughing, choking sound came from the little copse—a strangled, despairingly human cry—and then a bronze-skinned, four-limbed creature burst out opposite him.

Two great leaps and he had it.

He felt soft flesh, and the beast resisted fiercely. He released it quickly after a moment. For he saw that he had captured a female, clad as was he in a brief g-string of furry pelfhide, a short vest of the same material, and coarse, cracked sandals.

But—and his stomach rebelled with the horror of it—she too was a monster, like himself!

Instead of the two huge, muscular arms with which true Crus walked, ran, and worked, she had ungainly, tapering, long legs. And her arms, like his, were short and almost dainty, so soft was their appearance.

Like the lower animals of Ghakk, she used four limbs rather than two. She was atavistic—a throwback to the days when the Cru's ancestors were little better than beasts.

And yet it was comforting to know that another shared his own terrible deformity. Perhaps they could become friends and his ever-present sense of loneliness and self-loathing could be forgotten.

"Who are you, female-who-hides?"

The woman—and now he could see that her dark, dust-caked hair had hidden a dusky, even-featured face; a rather attractive face for a monster to possess—had stopped sneezing. Her teeth shone.

"I am Vanna. I come from the Valley of Jaff."

"Jaff?" He scratched thoughtfully at his gray-caked chest. "Never heard of it. Did they drive you out from among the Cru who dwell there?" He tugged at a lock of sandy hair.

"In a way." She laughed, and he liked the sound. He had never heard his mother laugh—but she had cried often enough, at the sight of him. "A Cruman and his three wives drove me out."

"How do you mean, er—Vanna?" He paused awkwardly. "By the way, I am Malan."

She bobbed her head pertly. "Well, you see, Malan, Jaff, who rules the Valley of Jaff, wanted me for his sixth mate."

"A Cruman wanted you—an ugly monster—for his mate?" Malan laughed scornfully. "It is a story you make up."

"I like that! I'm no more monster than are you."

"What I said. A monster like you and me. We should both have been destroyed."

The girl tapped her forehead. "Aren't you slightly off up here?" she asked, smiling. "But then, who isn't? I suppose I do look like a harpy."

"Are you being pursued, Vanna?"

"I expect so. Jaff and three of his five wives were hot on the trail last evening. But I traveled at night to throw them off."

"Through the cold?" The thought made Malan shiver. He had a single ragged blanket of pelf strapped on his back under which he would huddle in some warm cave nest.

Vanna tugged out two pelfskin robes that she had been sleeping on inside the little thicket's shelter, and showed them to Malan. She had laced them together to form a sort of furry nightshirt that reached to her sandals.

"It *was* cold," she admitted. "But better freeze than be beaten and abused by Jaff."

Malan twitched an eyebrow. The customs of the Crumen in her native canyon and his own obviously must differ widely. In the Valley of Cru even the mightiest warrior possessed but one mate. Nor would they consider allowing a monster in the valley, even as a slave.

He shrugged and hoisted the female monster's blanket to his shoulder. He could not stand here wondering and talking.

"Come," he said, turning and starting off. "We must not be captured."

Vanna stared after him, with anger, her slender little fingers caressing the dark wooden handle of the knife thrust through her g-string. She stood glowering, while he put a dozen paces between them.

"Why, that rock-headed brute!" she muttered to herself. "Never even asked me if I wanted to go that way!" She took a hesitant step.

Malan stopped, grinned back at her and waited.

"Your voice carries well," he said. "I think you're not really angry, are you?"

Vanna flashed a reluctant smile and shook her head ...

The last crimson streamers of Ghakk's ancient sun revealed the pursuing knot of warriors from the Valley of Cru.

The two fugitives were quitting a desolate dust flat, hill-rimmed and wide, and turned to look back. They saw ten of the Crumen come bounding, on tireless long arms, across the flattened gray expanse but a mile behind them.

Short they were, less than four feet in height, but broad of shoulder and long of arm. They were legless—only vestigial pads of feet with tiny nailless digits supported their humanoid trunks—but their upper limbs carried them along at a fast pace.

They carried throwing spears, bows, and short, metal-bladed swords. And most of them bore small packs in addition to the pouched harness about their bodies.

"We'll lose them among these rocks ahead," Malan promised doubtfully.

"What horrible-looking things they are, Malan."

Malan was thunderstruck. Had she never seen Crumen? He stared at her. "But they are Crumen," he said. "The Cru. We, you and I—are monsters."

"You poor gulpin," Vanna said. "Is that what they tried to tell you? In our valley we know the truth. True Cru have legs."

Malan made an expressive sound of disgust.

"Your people are mad," he said shortly. "Come, let us turn to the north and escape them."

They climbed for a time, the wind-rasped rock of the slope like coarse sandpaper under their clumsy sandals. They came to a ridge that angled northward, affording an easy path for a time.

The four tiny moonlets, racing close down to Ghakk's surface, were hidden as the last light from the sun died, but a few moments later the first pale satellite pushed above the eastern horizon. Now they could see where their stumbling feet were placed.

A second, and a third moonlet appeared. Light flooded the timeworn hills and ragged canyons and crevices. They quit the ridge and crossed a wind-swept apron of creviced rock to a second ridge. But they did not follow the easy way along the crest. The pursuing Crumen could not have failed to see a moving dot, or two dots, silhouetted by the moonlight upon the skyline. Malan knew better than that.

Vanna fell behind, limping. After a time she stumbled and fell. Malan came back and helped her up. He, too, was sagging with exhaustion.

"A little farther, Vanna," he whispered. "The canyon just below us is choked with huge boulders and fallen rimrock. Plenty of good hiding places—maybe caves."

"I'll make it, Malan."

Malan put his arm around her waist. The naked flesh was satiny and warm beneath his touch, and for the first time he felt a strange yearning emotion. He knew that she needed his help—that she accepted him as an equal—and he was content to serve her.

The pale moons sent blurred moving shadows racing before and beside them. They avoided sand and dusty patches of rock, trying to leave no spoor, as they struggled deeper into the rocky jumble.

It was bitterly cold, with their breath blossoming whitely in the thin air, when they found a rock-hidden tiny cave. There was sand on the floor, and into this they burrowed wearily.

Malan heaped the three robes over them and the female monster fell asleep with her head pillowed on his shoulder. A moment later and he, too, was dreaming.

Something was wrong. Malan was sure of it. He felt the coarse fluidity of the sand and the warmth of flesh other than his own. And his memory was dulled … What had happened?

His eyes opened.

He was looking up into the face of a female—a long-legged, monstrous female. And her face was familiar. It seemed—then he remembered. Vanna!

Yet at the same time he could feel a warm, unconscious body at his side, the gentle pressure of its breathing on his flesh, even and slow.

"You aren't Vanna!" And he groped for his knife.

The girl-shape wavered and became something else. A Cruman! No! A monster, for his legs were long and muscular. And his hair was sandy and hacked-off roughly about his ears. He looked like—he was—another Malan!

Malan knew a sudden paralyzing fear.

"A Shape!" he gasped.

Vanna stirred. Awoke.

The monstrous, changeable entity standing before them in the cave grinned in a friendly fashion. His weirdly familiar face shifted like a reflection in a disturbed pool and then steadied. Malan shuddered. Now the Shape would pounce …

He fought at the confining robes and at the hampering clasp of the terrified girl's hands. He felt the pelf-hide rending.

"Yes," agreed the grinning duplicate Malan, "I am a Shape. I am Rhee, fugitive from my own kind. And I would be friends."

Malan came surging up to his feet and grappled the creature. Rhee was unarmed and naked. But the body Malan seized was, at once, yielding and powerful. His arms were swallowed up, engulfed by the protoplasmic monster. He was helpless.

Vanna came at the Shape with her stone sliver of a knife bared. And all at once a whip of ropy flesh darted from the strange being's chest, to strip away the blade in her hand. She staggered backward and to her knees.

"Sorry to get rough with you two," Rhee said calmly. "But even a Shape takes little pleasure in having his flesh haggled by edged weapons."

"Eat us and be done!" flared Vanna, tears making her eyes bright. "We do not fear you!"

"I am not hungry, you silly mutant," the Shape said, chuckling happily. "I eat only vegetables, fruits, and fish. Are you any one of them?"

"Perhaps we were hasty," admitted Malan. "You could have eaten us both by now. But, among the Cru, it is said that the terrible Shapes eat one another."

Rhee released Malan. And behind the Shape the sun rode high in the heavens. Rhee squatted in the warm sunshine just inside the cave's entrance. He examined his right hand curiously. A second thumb grew as he stared.

"Oh, most of us are cannibalistic," he admitted with a smirk. "Many of my people have devoured as many as twenty of their own kin, or their own offspring. The food supply is rather uncertain in our valley, you see.

"But it happens that I am allergic to animal flesh. Huge purplish pustules break out over my entire body if I indulge, unfortunately. And, being a variant from the other Crumen, or Shapes, I was naturally forced to leave the valley and hide in these hills."

"Now," sighed Vanna, relief in her voice, "I can sleep nights. Providing, of course, that you join us."

"Never fear." Rhee grinned horribly again and changed into a pouchy-breasted old hag with stringy white hair. "I'll guard you from this forward young monster, dearie."

"Don't dearie me!" Vanna cried, her face flaming. "I'm not afraid of Malan. I just didn't want you nibbling off a leg or arm."

"My error, lovely mutant," said Rhee gallantly, bowing and switching abruptly again to his masculine form.

In his haste he forgot the scraggly white hair of the old female. It dangled like a hood of serpents down upon his brawny shoulders.

"Look, Rhee," said Malan uncertainly. "As long as a female is with us, and—well—hadn't you better hunt up a g-string or something?"

"Great jets, yes!" A gaudy reddish sash materialized, vanished, and was replaced by a hairy g-string. "I'd forgotten the silly regard you mutant monsters have for clothing."

"I suppose you Shapes never bother with garments?"

Rhee shook his head jerkily. "Nuh uh. We Crumen need no such coverings. Our outer flesh adapts to any temperature. Of course, you mutants find that impossible."

Vanna laughed scornfully. "You call yourself a Cru. And Malan calls the ugly legless ones Crumen, too. But my people, with our long legs and unchanging form, we are the *real* Crumen."

"What's the straight of it, Shape?" asked Malan, sorely puzzled. "Surely you must admit that we are all three monsters!"

Rhee scratched at his pale Medusa's locks with a thoughtful set of fingernails. The hair shortened and grew sandy again.

"The female is wrong—but so are you. Only a true Cruman could adapt himself to any form or environment, as we Shapes do."

A shadow, falling across Rhee's body, cut off Malan's possible reply. It was a short, compact shadow—legless!

"The Cru," rasped Malan, reaching for his bow.

Rhee fell in upon himself. He became a shapeless blob of writhing flesh and protoplasmic jelly. He flung out a thin whip of colorless, muscular flesh, and the legless one came thudding into their midst.

Malan quieted him with a fragment of rock. The warrior went limp. Malan stripped off his weapons and flung himself out of the cave.

A second legless one bounded toward them, on massive arms. His mouth opened to voice a triumphant cry. And then Rhee's whip of protoplasmic leathery flesh cut him down. Swift as Malan was, Rhee had preceded him out of the cave.

"Drag *it* out of sight," said Rhee, momentarily humanoid from the chest up, "and we'll polish off the rest of them quickly."

Malan dropped another rock against the bald brown skull and tugged the creature behind a huge boulder. There, with strips from the Cruman's blanket, he bound the mighty arms together.

"Rhee," he said huskily, "you're an all-right Shape." Swiftly he sprang back to the cave opening and ranged himself alongside his ally.

Malan, Vanna and Rhee were staggering under burdens of swords, water bladders and extra blankets as they climbed a ridge half an hour later. Behind them six weaponless, bound warriors chafed their bonds furiously against sharp rock edges. The Shape had roped them all very neatly.

"Without water," Rhee said, "they can follow no further."

"You know this country, Rhee," Malan said. "Where can we find a deserted and fertile canyon?"

The Shape laughed.

"Nowhere." He took up a fragment of chalky gray stone and knelt before a smooth, darker slab. "See, here is the Valley of Lizard Ones—the true Ghakkans, degenerate though they be. Directly north and west.

"West again from that is the double, U-shaped Valley of Shapes. And south of the Lizard Ones is the Valley of Giants—also mutant descendants of our race."

"No other valleys or little canyons that are habitable?"

"Two or three." Rhee nodded. "But monsters too horrible for the Cru or the other mutants to accept exist in them somehow. Hairy things, four, five—even eight-legged. Crawling blind things, yellow and slimy ..."

"What would you suggest then, Rhee?"

"I say let us cross the great fissure that bars this cut-up section from the land west of us. We don't know what lies beyond—desert or more badlands or fertile plains, or what kind of creatures—but it's worth a try."

Vanna nodded. "Sounds good to me. But how do we cross? Can you sprout wings and ferry us over?"

The Shape was amused. "I can glide for a short distance," he said, "but not carrying a load. However, there is one spot, south of the Valley of Shapes, where the great rift narrows to perhaps a hundred feet. There, three huge trees grow close together on the chasm brink."

"A bridge, eh?" Malan studied the map thoughtfully. "But here, so close to your people's valley, will we not be discovered?"

"It is a chance we must take, Malan. In the late afternoon we can risk it. Only in the morning do the Shapes hunt outside the barrier cliffs."

"I'm for it, Malan," Vanna cried out. "Once beyond the fissure, Jaff and his wives cannot follow us."

"I agree also, Rhee."

"Good," the Shape said, absentmindedly blossoming a cuplike bright blue ear from his chin momentarily, before he rose to lead the way.

So it was that they headed northward for a time, almost to the Valley of Lizard Ones. Toward evening they surprised a hunting party of six grotesque, brownish-scaled, dwarfish saurians, but the sight of them sent the upright little lizard men scampering.

And with night they found a low-roofed cave, with a narrow entrance, within which they built a fire.

"The Hairy Beasts," Rhee told them gravely, "may see the fire and come to attack us. However, as long as the fire burns the light will blind their weak pink eyes and restrain them."

"Why worry, then?" yawned Malan, and was asleep.

A second later, or so it seemed, he was dreaming that a Hairy Beast sat astraddle his chest. He felt the coarse hair rasping his naked flesh, and the stench of bestial breath was foul and hot in his face.

The dream was very real. He had experienced these nightmares before. He groaned disgustedly and attempted to roll over.

Abruptly he was fully awake. The weight was still there, and thick legs wedged his blanket-swathed arms to his sides. His eyes popped wide …

In the dying flare of the ashes he saw the gleaming, dagger-like teeth of the Hairy Beast close above his unshielded throat. They dropped nearer.

And Malan exploded into action, rolling out from under the apish brute, his arms rending the pelfskin blanket.

A second blanket splashed down over his head and body. He tore it away, stumbling over Vanna's sleeping body as he did so, and sprawling, headlong, into the embers of the fire.

He sprang upright again, cursing, and his eyes searched the shadowed cave for the misshapen brute.

The Hairy Beast had vanished. Rhee lay curled in his warm hides, his even breathing loud and undisturbed, and Vanna was sitting up, trembling. Perhaps he had injured her as well as frightened her! Her body was quivering in strange little spasms.

"Vanna," he said anxiously, sitting down beside her, while his eyes ranged the cave and its entrance. "I didn't hurt you?"

He pulled her extra blanket up around her shoulders and put his arm around her to reassure her. But the ugly, broken paroxysms continued—even more violently than before.

"Now, Vanna," he soothed. "Now, now!"

And then, as his mother had infrequently done—when she could conquer her natural revulsion at touching her monstrous son—he tipped up her face and gently kissed her. She quieted. He kissed her again.

It was pleasant. He had forgotten what loneliness was like; he had forgotten that they were both monsters fit only for destruction. He held her close to him for a long moment.

Vanna pushed him away. Her shoulders started jerking again, and now he saw that she was laughing. And that she had been laughing all the time …

"You looked so funny, Malan," she almost sobbed in hilarious agony, "when Rhee pretended he was a Hairy Beast!"

Malan gave her a disgusted shove. He started for Rhee's nest of blankets. But the Shape was gone.

Growling under his breath at the two jokesters, he settled again into his blankets. Swiftly his chilled body warmed, and he grew sleepy again. His last thought was how well Vanna's lithe body had fitted into his arms.

Vanna knelt beside him, her soft fingers caressing his eyelids. The morning sunlight shadowed her dark eyes and face as they shielded him from its flaming glow.

"I am ashamed of myself," she said tenderly, "that I angered you by laughing. Forgive me."

She bent lower. He flung aside the blankets and pulled her yet closer. Her lips parted …

"What's—what's all this?" a familiar voice cried out angrily from nearby.

It was Vanna. Malan sat up. And the Vanna that had melted so pleasantly into his arms, shifted, writhed, and became a laughing, toothless old crone with a twisted, warty chin.

Malan swung a knotted fist at the drawn lips and jutting chin, and felt a satisfying jolt travel up along his arm.

"A joke is a joke," said Vanna severely to the sprawled, but still cackling, Shape, "but there's a limit. From now on you better stay a Cruman—and with dark hair, too."

Rhee's masculine form returned, a glorious, muscle-rippling, deep-chested, godlike shape that made Malan feel like a boy. And the Shape's hair was a thick, tangled mop of black. He stood up.

"I'll try," he agreed, his strange new eyes shining like polished brass, "but I make no promises."

And for the next three days, while they traversed the desolate reaches of desert and empty, rock-strewn canyons, Rhee kept his word. Only once did he forget himself, and extend a fragile pseudopod to whisk an arrow from Malan's startled grasp.

As a consequence Malan was too late to down a shambling, bearlike pelf. And the slate-hued beast waddled hurriedly away among a cluster of eroded greenish boulders.

That was early in the third day, as they passed near the Valley of Giants, and well it was that they did not slay the pelf. For close on the heels of the clumsy brute came a score of the naked, hairy-headed giants.

Malan lay close beside Vanna in the shallow cup of sand-floored granite, with Rhee on her other side, and peered cautiously over the rim. A dead stub of cactus hampered full vision, but it also shielded his head from view.

Twice as tall as Malan were the pallid, elephantine monsters. Their heads were huge hairy masses of varied hues, from which only their tiny eyes and flabby red mouths and teeth gleamed. Many of them possessed extra rudimentary limbs, sprouting at random over their unlovely torsos, and two giants bore two fully developed heads apiece.

All of them carried knotted clubs in their misshapen fists.

"That was close," Malan muttered, after a long wait. "Did you see them or hear them coming, Rhee?"

"I should brag and say yes, Malan. The truth is, I was just being playful when I snatched that arrow from you."

"That evens you up for the other morning," said Vanna, still resentful.

"Malan hasn't dared to try kissing you since, eh?" Rhee chortled. "Anyhow, we'd have lost an hour dressing the pelf. And we might have reached the fissure too late."

"We must cross tonight?"

"Rather. The Valley of Shapes is too close at the point to take any chances. We might hide out until the following evening, but my people are skilled at scenting out any sort of edible flesh. Against more than one Shape we would be helpless."

"What's holding us back, then?" demanded Vanna, standing up and thunking her sandals into both their ribs. "Come on, you lazy ones!"

Three gigantic trees, white-boled and straight, with the rot of age hollowing out living caverns at their roots. Three forest giants, balanced on the sheer rift's brink, and lifting two hundred feet into the thin air of dying Ghakk …

Smoke, thin and pale, lifted from fires kindled on the chasm's side against their massive boles. In theory, the side first burned through would be the direction of fall. In practice—anything could happen.

They had decided to fell the three trees together, thus preventing any possible emulation of their bridging feat by others.

Vanna and Malan peered down into the great crack while the flames licked hotly upward behind them. A thousand feet—two thousand feet—perhaps much further, the emptiness fell away below. Darkness shrouded the murky depths, but a rock fragment, after a long interval, sent back the faintest echo of a splash.

All the face of Ghakk was split and riven in this fashion. Ghakk was a chilling, ancient planet circling a dark-shadowed luminary, and in her dying convulsions her outer husk was shattered.

Rhee joined them. "The trees' interiors are aflame now," he warned. "Once they topple we must hurry across."

Malan turned to watch the flames. He frowned doubtfully up at the growing column of heated air and smoke. Fortunately a stiff north breeze, from off the higher desert tableland they had quitted, caught it and ripped it apart. And the dust in the moving air merged with the smoke into a drifting haze.

"If we slip off the log," Rhee warned, "the ugly water-lovers, who dwell in the depths, will feast well. It is they who bar any descent into the sunken voids as a way of escape from this island of canyons."

"Are they, too, mutants?" Vanna wanted to know.

"No. When we Cru first came to Ghakk they were there. And long after we are gone the slimy amphibians will live on in their watery gulfs."

The fires crackled loudly. And the sun was nearing the western rim of the encircling uplands. In a few moments the sky would flame briefly with dusty sunset, and then darkness would come.

With a sudden loud cracking and popping of fibers the largest of the three trees started toppling—squarely out over the void!

"Perfect!" cried Malan.

The vast trunk smashed down, its bushy upper branches crashing and splintering on the opposite lip of the crevice. And then, with the slow, inexorable movement of heavy hinges, it buckled in the middle, and slid smoothly into the depths ...

Rhee grunted disgustedly, and his erect body slumped into something shapeless for one brief moment. Then he stood erect.

"Two to go," he said.

A moment. Two moments. And then the ominous crackling of the flames was drowned by the snapping explosions of wrenched and tortured wood. And now the two remaining trees leaned outward, together, and thundered down.

Hastily, the three moved well away from the vast cleft.

The upper limbs of the two trees meshed together and battled. The right hand tree revolved its fire-blackened bole and bounced toward the watchers. They dropped to the ground, cowering, and the ugly cylinder brushed across their prone bodies and was gone.

They saw the awesome bulk of it upending until it was vertical, as the crown plunged downward into the abyss. There was a rumble of sound and then nothing more.

The third tree remained, smoke curling from its rotten dry heart. And it seemed to be anchored securely in place.

"Still game, Vanna?" Malan's hand was on the girl's shoulder.

Vanna clung to his arm, put up her face to clear away the dark hair, and nodded. In the ebbing crimson twilight that had fallen he saw that her lips were thin over locked teeth.

"Take her over, Malan," came Rhee's urgent voice. "Those crashes may bring Shapes—or the tree may burn through."

Malan wanted to protest. He should cross first to see if all was safe. And then Vanna could follow. But there was an undertone of recognized danger that Rhee's voice revealed.

He helped Vanna up across the hot char to the white trunk. The bark was firm and free of scaly patches, but it was hot under their worn sandals. They hurried ahead, out over the emptiness. And now Malan was thankful for the growing dusk.

It was like running along a narrow, high-crowned road built above the level of a marsh or lake.

They reached the limbs, wriggled through and around them, and came at last to the solid rock beyond.

And when he had taken Vanna a safe distance from the mangled debris of the crushed limbs, Malan turned to go back to join Rhee. Only to see the Shape's indistinct body come springing lightly from the treetop.

"The base of the tree was almost burned through," he told Malan. "That is why I did not come with you. My added weight might have finished it off."

They backed away from the entangling branches. It was almost completely dark by now, although two of the wan little moons of Ghakk were lifting above the distant hilltops. They could see the red glow of the tree's blazing base.

The tree settled and crunched as though it was preparing for its fatal flight downward. Vanna cried out, pointing.

Four figures, monsters by the shape of them, were running toward them across the trembling bridge. The moons were waxing. Malan could see that one figure was that of a giant male and the others were females. And even as he watched the great bole shifted, sending a screaming figure gyrating madly into the depths below.

"Jaff and his mates!" cried Vanna, throwing herself into Malan's arms. She was sobbing.

Malan tore away her clinging fingers and pushed her aside, even while he unslung his bow and swung the quiver to a readier angle.

"Go back, Jaff!" he roared. "Vanna is my mate!"

A bull bellow of amused sound answered. The warrior waved muscular, hairy arms as he halted for a second.

"Not for long is she yours, dog-son," he jeered. "After I have crunched your skull and eaten of your heart she will be mine."

"Keep him talking," muttered Rhee. "The weakened trunk must break soon."

"Back!" cried Malan. "Go back. The tree is ready to crash!"

"Fool!" said Rhee. "Now he will try to rush us."

The warrior laughed derisively and came racing forward. Malan bent his bow and sent an arrow speeding toward that vague moving bulk. Another arrow—a third, and a fourth—and Jaff shrieked and went toppling through the branches he had but reached.

One of the females turned and went scampering back the way she had come, but the other came swiftly running toward them.

"Vanna!" she called out. "It is Nian!"

"She is not unfriendly," Vanna said. "Of all Jaff's mates she is the kindest—and the youngest."

Malan lowered his bow. He was wondering, thankful that the decision was not necessary, whether he could have killed the female monster. In his brain now was a sense of the difference between Crumen and their mates, a sense that was new to him. The females were to be protected—as he would always protect Vanna ...

Branches rasped across the bare rock. The ripping bark and leaves voiced a protesting groan, as the forest giant took its last plunge, and the female came catapulting out of the sky to the rocky ground before them.

The Shape dragged her limp body back from the brink of the chasm to safety.

It was noon, and the four who had crossed the crevice were entering the narrow entrance to a sparsely wooded valley. There was game here, and an hour before they had discovered a spring bubbling up through crystalline white sand.

All of them could live here, Malan was thinking. Here there need be no distinctions of monster or Cruman. His faith in the true Cru being the legless warriors from his home valley was badly shaken. Rhee, with his flexible adaptation to any shape and his ready wits, was certainly much superior to the legless ones.

And so, reluctantly, he was coming to regard the Shape as a Cruman, even as Rhee had claimed, while Vanna and Nian and he were obviously mutants. Vanna's claim that her tribe were true Cru was patently false—Nian was proof of that.

Nian moved gracefully, almost bonelessly, in front of them. Her long, fleshless limbs were double-jointed and flexible. A second pair of tiny pale blue eyes were set close to her narrow blade of a nose, below her wide great eyes of deepest violet. She was long-faced, with tiny white teeth, and the orange-red of her hair sprouted in weird tufts.

There was the unhuman beauty of a wild creature about her …

They rounded a sweeping wall of reddish shale and rotten yellow rock, and looked across a dry-crusted swale to where a shallow, mile-wide lake opened. From the calm, dark waters a weird rounded mass loomed.

"The spassip!" Malan cried out.

He was dazed. The legend of the spassip that had brought the Cru to Ghakk, a legend he had scarcely believed, was suddenly to become reality. The vastness of the mile-long ship awed him. It was like a hill spanning the lake.

Just before them, a ready finger of mud extended outward toward the crumpled nose of the spassip. Already the Shape and the monster female, Nian, were racing fleetly across it.

Vanna and Malan followed.

Rhee was climbing through one of the rust-stained gaps in the ship's upper hull. He paused long enough to lend Nian a ropy tentacle, and pulled her up after him. Then they both vanished into the interior.

A moment later Malan was assisting Vanna through the same opening into a twisted, dust-floored corridor with walls of distorted metal. The broken webs of fist-sized *chedda* spiders marked the passage of Rhee and Nian. They followed.

On either hand strange metal caves, dusty and choked with debris, opened. They saw strange furnishings of metal and sleek horn-like material.

They came at last to the dusty, dimly lighted control room, where the three brave Cru of that age-old legend had died, and they reverently examined the corroded control panels and ruined equipment.

Rhee turned from a metallic drawer, a rounded metal plate in his hand, and stalked woodenly over to Malan. Wordlessly, he passed the little medallion to the monster.

Malan studied the raised figures and the odd lettering.

"Monsters," he said, wonderingly, "like Vanna and me."

Rhee shook his head, his features fluid and smoothly empty. And there was a listlessness in the motion that chilled Malan. The truth came flooding into his brain.

He saw the sprawled, dust-coated space suit in which a Cruman had died, and it had long separate legs. Another plaque of dull metal on the wall showed two long-legged creatures standing with clasped hands. In the background loomed a spassip, on which strange symbols were inscribed.

"The Second Ark." Malan examined the cryptic, meaningless letters. But he knew the truth now. He knew at last that it was he, he who was a true Cruman, as was Vanna. They two alone were true descendants of the fabulous, brave people who had traveled from some distant planet to Ghakk in this ship. The Shape, the Giants, and the Legless Ones—all of them were mutants.

So now was Rhee to be considered a "monster"? A true comrade, with a wisdom beyond his own, who had treated him as an equal even though he had then been classed a mutant …?

He flung an arm around the Shape's shoulder.

"All the monsters," he said, "we left across the rift."

And Vanna was smiling agreement. This time it would be different. Mutant and Cru would work shoulder to shoulder to build a life for themselves, to fashion a world where they might be happy and safe …

Ship of the Fog Seas

The great metal shield that was Sky Island—largest of the ten artificial satellites circling Terra—was expanding below the *Mallory*. In a matter of minutes the battered old space freighter would warp into one of the loading docks and discharge her meager freight of Martian artifacts and uranium.

"In a few minutes I leave this ancient pig sty forever," said dour little Pierre Mercier, Ralph Brett's second aboard the freighter.

He snapped his fingers at the captain, a sneer on his sallow, narrow features. "And you as well, my officious superior."

Brett smiled at this gentle—for Mercier—remark.

"The feeling is mutual," he agreed. "Anything I can do to speed you on your way?"

At that instant the interior of the aged spacer seemed to convulse and turn inward upon itself. There was a brittle snapping, more mental than physical. The lights dimmed …

And then the lights were bright again and the low throb of the control jets sounded throughout the ship.

Brett shook his head vigorously, his eyes slowly becoming unblurred. He checked the visuals—blinked in disbelief. Apparently there were two auxiliary, and smaller, suns in the inky heavens!

Sky Island had disappeared, nor was there any trace of the other nationalistic satellite ports nearby. Terra was as naked of satellites as she had been two centuries before—only Luna was left to her.

Terra itself was changed. He could see strange mountains and belts of foggy looking atmosphere hiding the oceans and plains.

"What is it, Brett?" Mercier demanded. "Why are we not near the satellite docks? A space eddy perhaps?"

"A space warp or a time warp, I'm afraid, Mercier. Terra seemed so terribly changed—perhaps we have even been hurled into a dimensional parallel cosmos!"

"Space wash," Mercier scoffed. "Other-dimensional-continuum-fairy-tales were forgotten before the Twenty-First Century."

"I know. Science wrote off the space warp and the time warp as fantastic too. But we know different."

The only passenger aboard the freighter, Kathryn Train, leaned forward in her padded landing chair. She shook the tousled blonde curls out of her eyes. Bright intelligent eyes they were, Brett remarked wordlessly—for perhaps the thousandth time ...

"This wouldn't be the first ship to suddenly vanish in space," Kathryn said unsteadily. "Even on the surface, ships and people disappear quite frequently."

"That's right, Mrs. Train. Maybe we'll meet up with some of them. Now I'll try to set our ship safely down on this planet—and possibly we can find out what it is all about."

He indicated the fog-misted globe on the control visuals.

"Don't be a fool, Brett," cried Mercier. "We're almost out of fuel. We must fall into an orbit until help arrives. We'll crash if we try landing."

"Rescue is out of the question. Our only hope is to find a livable environment at once, Mercier. So get after the skimmers and milk their fuel tanks dry. Jettison the cargo—put Strang to work on that at once."

"But—the fuel won't ..."

"Mister Mercier!" Brett interrupted angrily. "Carry out my orders."

Still grumbling to himself Mercier left the control room. The burly mech technician, Peter Strang eased out of his strapped seat and stood up. He was a heavy-set man with tiny piggish green eyes that peered insolently from beneath bushy dark eyebrows.

"All the cargo, Strang, and surplus skimmers—after Mercier has stripped them. Retain only two of them—four and seven. Also dump the emergency space cells.

"We'll coast down at the shallowest possible angle, trying to slow our speed by atmospheric friction. If it were not that we might need the ship, I would favor abandoning it and using the skimmers, but this planet may be waterless or have a poisonous atmosphere—and we may be forced to live aboard ship."

Kathryn Train, to whom his last remarks had been made, nodded her understanding. "Anything I can do to help?" she asked.

Kathryn was slightly younger than Brett and fluidly rounded in a graceful feminine way. He was forced constantly to remind himself that she was married to a minor company executive of *Sol Transport*.

"Tie down anything you value, Mrs. Train. It may be a rough landing. And put extra shock cords on your emergency hammock. Maybe extra clothing for padding—and lace this brace around your neck."

"It sounds terribly dangerous—and awfully romantic, Captain. Looks as though we might be stuck here for life. What about that understanding you have with—Helen, isn't it? And me, I may never see Waldo again unless a miracle occurs."

"At the moment the most pressing problem is landing safely," Brett said dryly, not quite sure if she were really as callous toward her husband as she seemed, or if she were merely trying to keep up her spirits.

The wet denseness of atmosphere had come about them and they rode a few thousand feet above the slow-boiling surface of the foggy clouds. To the south the majestic loom of east-west, snowy mountains rose in great steps skyward.

The ship was coming in fast to a sort of plateau, or island, that lifted above the all-pervading clouds. According to Brett's calculations this spot approximated the same latitude and longitude on this strange world as did his native state of New York on Terra.

The plateau appeared to be less than fifty miles in diameter, a rough platter of vegetation, barren rock, and water. Near its center gleamed a lake, about four miles long and half as wide.

"Have to ditch her in the lake, or near it," Brett told Kathryn.

All four of them were laced into their shock hammocks for protection against the impending crash. Kathryn smiled weakly to show that she had heard. Strang's jaws were locked and his eyes slitted, but Mercier was visibly terrified. Tears were streaking his dirty cheeks, and his lips were trembling.

Now they saw that a small city lay to the east of the lake, along a small, deep cut bay. It was surrounded by a low massive wall and contained many parks and wide streets. Most of the buildings appeared to be low domed structures.

One other peculiarity of the plateau was the deep valley, or foggy bay, that cut ten or twelve miles into the eastern rim almost to the lake's outlet.

With a last feeble gasp of rocket fuel Brett braked the old space freighter and grounded her less than half a mile from the city. She plowed through a reedy marsh, leaving a twisted muddy canal behind her, and came to rest less than a hundred yards from the lake's outlet.

"Better than I expected," Brett said. He helped Kathryn out of her hammock and turned to the two others.

"Break out the super mechs, Mercier, and put the work mechs to hauling material for a turbo generator. Looked like a very considerable waterfall at the lake's outlet.

"Strang, you check over our accumulators and prepare them for recharging. Later we'll find some way to refine shale or some other type of fuel for the skimmers."

The two men hesitated in the control room lock.

"And I suppose you'll be playing Venusian *skeesh* with the passenger while we work," sneered Mercier.

Brett stood up and moved swiftly to Mercier. His hand twisted the tunic around the latter's throat.

"I'd like nothing better than to push in your teeth," he said coldly. "But that can wait. Until we are all safe you will be respectful to both Mrs. Train and myself."

"I—I understand, sir." Mercier's face was turning black. "Please. I'm ... I'm ..." Brett released his grip. "... sorry."

"Mrs. Train and myself will use two of the mechs to scout the city," Brett said, "providing, of course, that she has used *mentrols* before."

Kathryn laughed. "Of course I have. Waldo and I spent several weeks exploring Io and Europa last year. And I was pleased to learn that two of your super mechs are female—makes me feel more at home."

"Kath—Mrs. Train will use Jill. Mercier can take Blacky, and Strang can use Tubby. One of the other two mechs is broken. Is it Suzy or Jack, Strang?"

"Suzy," the mech technician grunted. "Jack's in good shape."

Aboard any spaceship, whether freighter or passenger, the super mech is indispensable. With a controlled robot, repairs can be made while in flight—protracted exposure in a spacesuit to the deadly actinic radiations of deep space is invariably fatal to a human being—and for exploration on poisonous, dangerous, superheated or frigid planets the super mech is absolutely necessary.

Not for several days would the crew of the *Mallory* dare venture outside the ship. There were tests to make and explorations to be carried out before it was proven safe. Until then the half-ton robots would carry on all outside activities.

They went together to the cabin where the five mentrol units, with their comfortably cushioned sleeping plates beneath them, were placed. The mass of mentrol equipment shared the cabin with banks of speech analyzers, viewing and recording files, and their meager arsenal of two rocket rifles, two paralysis pistols, and a hand machine gun that expelled explosive needles.

Mercier and Strang were already reclining on their plates, letting the transparent hoods lower down upon their heads and shoulders, when Brett and Kathryn arrived. Brett showed Kathryn to the unit controlling Jill and then found his way to his own resilient sleeping plate.

He lowered the hood, felt the contacts' flexible pressure on his skull and neck, then jabbed at the toggle to set the power humming through all the circuits.

Brett felt the faint shock he always experienced when he used the mentrols and became aware that he was looking through other eyes and feeling with other tactiles. He had used the robots a thousand times before—yet never could he overcome that sensation of awe and disorientation.

He was seven feet of stalwart male humanoid, so realistically constructed that true humans might well mistake him for one of themselves. Jack, as he now identified himself, moved. He stepped forward out of the retaining clamps into the third and inmost airlock, then out through locks two and one toward the lake. A moment later, Jill, a magnificent, dark-haired giantess, joined him.

All afternoon the super mechs and the ordinary robots worked at installing the turbine. The seven work mechs amused Kathryn, as she waited for Brett to join her on the scouting mission. Their awkward repetitious actions were almost pathetic. They were squat, round-bodied affairs, six feet in diameter, with a single broad caterpillar tread instead of legs. They constantly needed manual control, despite the automatic relays which should have eliminated too great a breakage of parts. They looked very stupid and acted like poisoned beetles.

After the generator was installed and power flowing to the spaceship, Brett and Kathryn—in the robot bodies of Jack and Jill—set off across the brilliant greensward to explore the silent city. Brett carried an axe as his only weapon.

The ancient roadway was yellowish, narrow, and rubbery. It led through a wide opening into an empty and long-abandoned city where shrubs and stunted trees rooted into the creviced black walls.

At one time there must have been gates, but they were long gone now. The walls were thirty feet thick at the base and lifted almost as high. Vines, thorny bush, and twisted gray-barked trees choked the side streets, but the wide avenue they followed was remarkably free of living debris.

Only an occasional patch of purple moss marred the smooth yellow way.

They passed great domes that seemed untouched by time. On both sides were crumbling windowless walls like red and yellow canyon cliffs. Huge weatherworn statues of six-limbed, vaguely humanoid beings lined the way.

"The City Builders," mused the girl, her super mech's brows drawn together in concentration. "Three suns … seas of fog … mountains and plateaus lifting above them …"

"Strike a familiar note somewhere, Kathy?"

"Mmm. Something I read before we left Toronto, or after we moved to Long Island. One of the ancient books Waldo was always bringing home … blue cover—thick book with a thousand or so pages—sun had faded part of cover almost white."

"Probably a collection of some sort. Historical or fantastic?"

They had passed through the city by now, and their pace quickened as the gateway fell behind them. Less than a mile ahead the foggy bay beckoned.

Kathryn had not answered his question, but now, abruptly, she laughed triumphantly.

"Fantasy," she said. "That was the clue I needed. 'Ancient Myths of Other Worlds.' That was its title. It tore apart all the myths from Atlantis and Lemuria down to the Twenty-Second Century."

"So this is a myth!"

"Maybe. Anyway the book dealt with the queerly persistent myths of parallel universes or dimensions sharing the same space … and in particular the myth of a linked world called Thrane. A fiction writer of the Twentieth Century is credited with its creation—and for spreading such a belief."

"Thrane, you said. Sounds familiar. Think I read something about it once. Something about it containing fog seas, near the boiling point, with strange six-limbed entities dwelling in massive-walled cities in their depths. Fairy tales."

Jill gestured back toward the dead city.

"Well, isn't that a pretty good imitation? And there were supposed to be gateways to other linked worlds—to some ten or fifteen, and one of them was Terra."

"Oh yes, I remember that now, Kathy. Sure. Earthmen were supposed to have gone through by the thousands, most of them unwillingly, until the First Atomic War. After that the gateways were blasted shut—sealed forever."

"That's it!" Kathy said excitedly. "Somewhere to the south of us are the plateaus where they settled—if the old myths were actually true."

"Sure—only a few hundred miles. Want to ski across—or would you prefer to swim?" Brett asked sardonically.

They were close to the abrupt ending of the highroad. Another two hundred paces and the fog sea would open below them. Jill placed her large capable hands on Jack's shoulders. They faced one another.

"You'll think of something," she said. "All we need is fuel for the skimmer."

"That's all," agreed Brett.

"And once we're on the mainland perhaps we can reopen the gateways from this parallel universe. The artificial eddies which created these openings were permanent—only their approaches are sealed off."

"According to the myths," said Brett ironically. "Come on, Kathy. Let's go on to the brink."

A moment later they were standing on the rim of a stupendous chasm. V-shaped it was, a great gouge cut out of the island's circular green plate. Its lower slopes, sheer and wooded, went down—down, until the fog sea lapped wispily against them a mile or more below.

"It's terrifying." The feminine super mech swayed as she spoke.

Brett put out a sustaining arm as she teetered on the edge of that terrible gulf. She sagged against his arm helplessly for a long moment. And the soft warmth of her vibrant synthetic body stirred his distant human blood.

To Brett, Jill *was* Kathy—and only the realization that she was the wife of another, prevented him from kissing the moist red lips.

None too gently he lowered Jill to the resilient roadway. And then he moved away several paces to stand on wide-spraddled legs, with the gusty damp wind from below warm on his sensitive pseudo-flesh.

He peered southward across that darkening gray plain of seething fog. The three suns were setting in the west, and the lone moon of Thrane was a hand's breath above the horizon's level rim.

Across there, if this was indeed the world of myth, lay fertile plateaus, descending in hundred-mile wide steps from stupendous snowy mountains. And on those plateaus men from Terra—and from other linked worlds—had built their cities.

"We'll cross it somehow," he said savagely.

Ten days later he dumped the first fourteen gallons of vegetable oil, pressed from the luxuriant mat of blue-veined vines that grew beneath the fog sea's misty roof, into the skimmer's empty fuel tanks.

The vine, which Kathryn uncertainly identified as *agan*, was rich with oil. And the further they descended into the terrific heat of the lower slopes, the more plentiful the vine became.

The super mechs and the standard mechs experienced no difficulty withstanding the sweltering temperature. They set up presses and still, and the slow process of filling the tanks began.

It was slow and wearisome work. An eight-hour hitch at the mentrols dulled their senses and left them with a raging headache. They took more frequent rests, and even ventured outside the *Mallory* to breathe the clean pure air of Thrane, and to swim in the central lake. The brunt of the work fell on Kathryn and Brett.

"At this rate," Kathryn sighed, slipping off her mentrol hood and sitting up on the sleeping plate, "we'll be here another two or three months."

"Hardly that." Brett handed her a greenish glass of *stym* and lighted her cigarette. "We're just getting into production. And the lower we go the more oil content. Say two weeks—maybe less."

"I hope you're right. I should be enjoying this island's beauty and peace. But I feel something sinister. Maybe it's the way Mercier and Strang look ..."

"You're imagining ghosts," Brett broke in. He nodded his head violently toward the intercom. The other two members of the ship's crew could hear every word. "It's that deserted city."

Kathryn crushed out her cigarette, her nod of understanding eloquent, and then she shrugged her shoulders as she slid again under the mentrol hood.

Brett finished his greenish stym and followed suit.

To find himself lying on his face in the steaming foulness overlaying the slimy carpet of agan roots.

His arms were lashed behind him and linked with the cords about his legs. Some unsuspected enemy had fastened him so securely that even his more-than-human strength could not break free without damage. To part the many strands restraining him would strip away the carefully built-up network of synthaflesh, nerve cells, and pseudo-blood channels.

Until he knew more about his captors, he preferred not to take this course.

He arched his back and snapped over to a half-sitting position. His eyes probed the gray semi-twilight of the fog sea until he saw Jill's nearby bound form, sprawled face down.

Feet and ivory-skinned legs came crowding about them. The feet were four-toed and webbed, and thong-bound sandals covered the soles.

His eyes traveled upward. He saw sturdy, thick-set bodies clad in a sort of thin leather jerkin and a loin cloth of similar material. About their middle they wore wide leather belts that supported sheathed, double-edged swords of bronze, or some similar alloy, and an ugly assortment of greenish metallic knives.

At their hips, wrinkling the leather jerkin, projected two stubby limbs, with four digits on each—which seemed to be neither fingers or toes. Above that they were definitely humanoid, with full reddish-black lips, thick-lidded purple eyes, and pointed, broad-based ears, with a crest of wavy bluish-yellow tendrils lifting a foot above their well-shaped skulls.

Brett set the speech analyzers to maximum reception and let Jack slump down again. Then he withdrew. He slid off the plate and shook Kathryn.

"Snap out of it, Kathy. Leave Jill as she is. Perhaps we can rescue both of the super mechs before they are damaged."

Kathy nodded, her blue eyes startled.

He contacted Mercier and Strang on the intercom and explained the situation.

"I plan to go after them with Tubby and a paralysis pistol. If I haven't returned by the time the repairs on Blacky have been completed, I expect one of you, preferably Mercier, to follow."

Brett turned to the girl, who was tugging at his elbow.

"I'm taking over Jill," she said, "so we'll know what's happening."

Brett hesitated. "Okay. But withdraw quickly if they attempt torture or murder. The transmitted shock can kill."

"Check," agreed the girl. "Be seeing you."

Brett hurried to Tubby's sleeping plate and lowered the mentrol hood. He sent Tubby slamming out of his restraining clamps and racing down the ramp from the locks toward the city.

Tubby was thick-bodied and clumsy looking. A series of recorded and unrecorded mishaps had badly warped his frame. He moved as unevenly and jerkily as a crippled crab. Even so his speed approached the mile a minute mark as he dashed through the streets and came to the island's upper rim.

Down the crooked trail they had marked out he hurried, thankful for the tough vines and poles they had anchored along the worst stretches. More than once they saved the lurching old robot from disaster.

He plowed past the ever-busy bulbous work mechs on the wide barren bench of reddish rock, and dodged the oil press and the filled drums of oil. And so he came at last to the lower shelf, far below the fog sea's surface, where Jack and Jill had been gathering agan for the press.

The two super mechs were gone.

He found a crushed trail through the slimy pale undergrowth and exposed roots left by the six-limbed natives. He followed their spoor downward until the last faint patch of sunlight merged into a dull gray blanket of fog. The heat must have been terrific—according to Tubby's patched-together gauges the boiling point of water was long since passed.

Brett emerged suddenly from a root-clogged waterway that served as a stairway upon a sandless rocky beach of wave-scoured dark rock. Steaming waves curled in and smashed against the shore; the murky water was thick with a jellied purplish growth.

Fifty feet offshore, the limit of even his superior vision, he made out the misty outlines of a broad, decked-over craft. Two rows of jutting oars and a thick-boled stubby mast were also visible. Now he heard the creak of a poorly lubricated windlass as the anchor was hoisted.

He sent Tubby sloshing into the flurry of creaming waves, since super mechs normally were capable of operating for days, even weeks, under water, provided there was no interference with the power-flow from the mentrols.

Six great steps he took—and froze! Water sloshed and battered about his shoulders. Only the crippled super mech's left arm continued to function. With this he managed to drag the inert robot body, somehow, back upon the rocky beach. There the super mech sprawled helplessly.

And the ship vanished into the foggy sea.

The ensuing week was a busy one.

Brett discarded Mercier's plan to pursue the ship in the partially fueled skimmer. Instead they babied and coddled the remaining super mechs into gathering more agan.

The supplies of oil were reaching comfortable proportions. The spaceship's accumulators were almost fully charged—capable of maintaining the ordinary routine of ship life for a hundred days or more.

Only the continued silence of the radio worried Brett. If this were Thrane and the stories of civilized men settling here were true, why was there no response to their radioed signals for help?

Could the colonists have fallen into barbarism or been destroyed by some alien scourge or conquering race?

Brett and Kathyrn kept in close touch with their captured super mechs. And Jack's hookup with the speech analyzers was paying off. They could now understand the speech of the humanoid natives who sailed the hidden seas of Thrane.

Tarv Gan, the ship's captain, was taking these strange four-limbed creatures to the city of Gorda to exhibit them there, and Gorda was on the mainland.

The Thranian was puzzled at their lack of energy—he had seen them ripping the agan stems apart as though they were rotted tissues. He kept them securely bound, however, although he did not permit his crew to abuse them lest they die and become valueless.

Now, with the skimmer's tanks full enough for a thousand miles of flight, Brett was checking for the last time on the condition of Jack and

Jill. And with him was Kathyrn. They relaxed on the sleeping plates, watching and talking quietly.

They were discussing the projected flight to the mainland.

"Why go alone, Ralph? Let me go along. I can pilot a skimmer."

"Too risky. What would your husband say if he learned I risked a passenger's life—your life—needlessly?"

"Oh, bother!" Kathryn's voice was shrill. "I divorced Waldo while we were on Europa."

"That's news," Brett said dryly. "Funny you never mentioned the divorce before. You can't get around me by lying, Kathy."

In the ensuing silence Brett could almost see the girl's lips pout. He grinned. If only Kathryn's suddenly announced divorce were real ... He knotted his fists. Why shouldn't he tell her how he felt about her? After all, the old familiar universe was doubtlessly gone forever.

"I don't want to be left here with Strang," Kathy was saying. "Or with Mercier, either. They give me the creeps."

"That's warpy, Kathy." Brett was very conscious of the intercom and the possibility that both men were listening. "They're no more dangerous than I am."

"Don't feed me that!" she snapped. "I know you better than ..."

The mentrol hood came jamming down upon his shoulders, pinning him there. He felt hands, and then thin tough cords, as he was bound securely to the sleeping plate. The mentrols clicked off, then, and the hood was lifted.

Strang was glaring down at him, his single bushy eyebrow quirked above the red blob of his shapeless nose. Now he laughed, showering the helpless space pilot with alcoholic saliva.

"Figured to leave the three of us here to rot, huh?"

Brett twisted on the sleeping plate until he could see Kathryn. Pierre Mercier held both her hands and was slapping tough brown packaging tape around her wrists. He felt the rising surge of blood pound angrily in his ears. His muscles tensed and he strained at his bonds.

"This is mutiny, Mercier," he said tonelessly.

Mercier's yellowish little teeth shone briefly. He bowed.

71

"I cannot agree. Your authority was ended when we came through the dimensional eddy or whatever it was. This is not Terra."

"The ship is Terran, Mercier. Even in an alien universe. Better turn us loose."

Mercier laughed hysterically. His eyes were glassy and he swayed unsteadily on his slender legs. Apparently he had been drinking too much and too swiftly, and this had touched off his smoldering hatred and rebellion.

Strang spat on the deck.

"You been hoggin' the dame," he snarled. "Now we get our turn."

"So that's it. Don't be fools. Mrs. Train will tell you how wrong you are. There is nothing between us."

"She'd lie. I know women. Flamers and cradle-rockers—they're all alike. But we're taking her with us—to the mainland."

"Would you take her against her will, Mercier?"

Mercier blinked, then grinned vacuously.

"Sure. This isn't Terra." He belched. "Make m'own laws."

Kathryn's laughter burst out suddenly. An amused carefree trill.

"Good, Pierre," she said. "I wondered when you would wake up and act like a man."

Brett felt his stomach knot uncontrollably. Even Kathryn was turning against him.

"This—this *person*," she said, glaring at Brett, "ordered me to keep away from both of you."

"But you said nothing—never even looked at me," objected Mercier.

"With that—wretch always snooping?" Kathyrn laughed sarcastically. "And both of you under his thumb? Hardly!"

Mercier shook his head wonderingly. He shook it long and violently. Brett, for a brief moment, wondered if this might not be some burlesque on a mutiny cooked up by Kathryn and Mercier. Then he realized that both crewmen were intoxicated—Mercier to the verge of helplessness.

"Cut me loose and let's get out of here," Kathryn urged. "I'm sick of looking at this character."

She scowled at Brett—and almost imperceptibly her right eyelid quivered in a faint shadow of a reassuring wink. Brett's despair vanished. Kathyrn might pull it off. She hadn't turned on him after all.

Mercier clumsily stripped off the tape. Kathryn preceded them into the corridor. He heard the locks clash, felt the faint suction of moving air, heard them clang again. A lock thudded a third time, followed by a series of faint thumps. Then he heard the sound of feet racing towards the mentrol cabin.

It was Kathryn. Swiftly she freed him with a machete-like jungle knife from the lockers. Then she scooped up a paralysis pistol and headed for the locks again.

"Quick!" she cried. "Those drunken fools will be taking off."

Brett jerked a rocket rifle from its springlastic clips and followed. He was close upon her heels as they emerged from the outer lock and started racing toward the skimmer. Even as they did so, however, the ship lurched drunkenly about on thrumming jets. It shot off the ground, dipping and skipping and splashing its way across the lake's surface. Brett dropped the butt of the rocket rifle on his toes without realizing it.

"Automatic pilot, you utter fools!" he shouted.

The hedge-hopping ended abruptly, as though they had heard and heeded. The ship climbed steadily and headed southward across the fog sea toward the mainland. Brett gave utterance to a sigh of relief.

"They should make it safely—if they can land. And when they sober up they may return."

"I wager they never come back," Kathryn cried angrily, as she leaned against Brett's arm. "They know we'll be armed and waiting. They'll hide the skimmer and disappear."

"You could be right, Kathy. I hope this was all unplanned, but I wouldn't want to gamble on that, either. The radio may have been damaged purposely—and this may have been brewing ever since we landed."

"Well, don't stand there like a space goon, Brett. Let's check up and see."

Ten minutes later, Brett nodded grimly at the girl.

"Sabotaged, and cleverly too. Take a few days to repair it—knowing as little about it as I do."

"That leaves Jack and Jill. The boat is almost ready to dock. If we could break loose, take over the ship and gain the mainland, we might recapture the skimmer."

"A remote possibility. But the other skimmer is without fuel, and probably wrecked, besides ... we'll make our break when the boat docks at Gorda. Isn't that better than while at sea?"

"Perfect, Ralph."

"Of course that still leaves us stranded on this island—with our super mechs on the mainland."

"Not if we can find the skimmer. And even if we can't, perhaps we can find the towns of the Earth settlement. Anyway, with those two rats gone, this island isn't so bad. I'll hate to leave it, after all."

Brett swallowed audibly. He was suddenly uncomfortably warm—and acutely aware of Kathy's nearness.

With effort, he controlled himself and headed for the locks.

"I'll contact Jack," he told the girl, "while you pilot Tubby, Blacky, and the regular robots up from the press."

"Right," agreed Kathryn cheerfully. Her blue eyes were alive with dancing mischief. "And then we'll drink some stym and sit around enjoying a little vocowire music. Maybe dance a little, huh?"

"I'm afraid we'll be too busy for such amusements for a time, Mrs. Train," he said stiffly.

A moment later he was adjusting the mentrol hood down over his head and shoulders, and wondering why it was that the only woman he had ever learned to love already had a husband. She seemed to enjoy making him squirm, too—leading him on in a most unsportsmanlike manner ...

Then he was sprawled in the filthy dank cabin where the half-ton bodies of Jack and Jill had been flung.

The ship dipped and swung, the deck groaning beneath him. Jill's inert, gracefully tapered legs were draped nudely across his own sturdier lower limbs. He could see that the many cords which bound her were burrowed deep into her smooth bronzed synthaflesh.

He inched his body along the deck until he had wriggled and twisted half around and his teeth were tight against Jill's bound hands. Then he began to gnaw at the soggy rawhide bands. The leather parted easily. In less than five minutes Jill's limp arms were free. Now he would switch sleeping plates and use Jill to free Jack.

Abruptly there came the sounds of trampling and shouting above deck. For a moment Brett thought that the harbor of Gorda must be at hand. Then he distinguished some of the Arban words.

"Pirates!" they were shouting. "… off the port bow! Bring nets … Heat the oil … Repel boarders!"

Sailors scurried to and fro outside the narrow door of the cabin, their arms laden with broad-bladed swords and knife-tipped pikes. Some carried crude nets to be hurled down to entangle their foes. The scent of scorching oil grew until it was a foul stench.

Brett switched off his mentrols and sprang over to Jill's hooded plate. Kathryn was busy controlling Tubby, so he shouted at her:

"Kathy!" And when her hood lifted, he added: "Drop that! I've freed Jill. We're in trouble. Come on!"

Then he was sitting up in the ship's cabin. He was immediately conscious of the finer texture of his synthetic flesh and its awkward feminine shape.

There was no time to lose. From the toolbox within what should have been Jill's thoracic cavity he took a pair of thin metal shears. With these he set about freeing Jack's cord-wound torso.

Even as the last length of rawhide fell away Jack came alive.

It was confusing to realize that this bronzed, broad-shouldered male was controlled by a woman's intelligence.

"What now, Ralph?" Kathy asked, in the definitely manly tones of Jack's voice pattern.

"The pirates seem to be getting the upper hand. I prefer the ship's crew to them. Tarv Gan seems a decent sort."

"Agreed. So we help the crew?"

"What else can we do? The pirates may want to heave us over the side or let us sink when they scuttle the ship. Besides, they probably aren't headed for the mainland."

"Roger, Mr. Brett. Lead me to a club or a sword."

Brett tossed a four-foot roller of scarred wood, used in stowing bulky cargo, to her and took a similar weapon for himself.

"Keep away from the ship's rail. We both weigh too much to swim ashore. We'd sink like stones."

"That's fine with me. This gal hates swimming, anyhow."

They dashed out into the ship's open waist. The confusion and carnage was indescribable. All the rowers' benches were empty—empty of living men, that is. A deepening pinkish color was growing in the sloshing half-floored bilge. There were broken reddish lumps that struggled and mewled insensately underfoot.

Brett raced up the wide wooden steps to the forward deck. Steps splintered and crunched beneath Jill's mighty weight, but he gained the deck. Jack came pounding along close behind.

He caught a glimpse of three low, single-banked galleys, lashed close together under the larger ship's overhanging bow. And swarming across the deck came a flood of scarred, cursing Arbans, swords and knives in all four of their hands.

It was like facing a buzz-saw. Already the pirates had chewed through the pike-wielding sailors.

Jack and Jill charged into the affray, their weighty billets of wood thudding and crunching. They swept the pirates overboard like so many crippled flies. The battle for the ship quickly became a rout. The super mechs seemed invulnerable.

Jack did lose a square inch of earlobe, and had a bloody slash along his cheek which Kathryn could not explain later. Jill was blessed with a beautiful purple-and-yellow eye where the handle of a hurtling sword had landed.

The makers of super mechs were sticklers for realism.

The pirates fell back to their boats in a panic. Two of the galleys fended free, but the boiling oil with which the crew now deluged them, caused those in the third galley to jump overboard.

When it was all over, Tarv Gan, the broad-faced ivory captain of the ship, came to them and bowed low—backward.

"Anything," he said humbly. "Anything I can do for you is yours. And pray forgive the cruelty I have done you both. My life, my cargo, my ship—all of them have you saved."

"Then put us ashore at once," Brett said in the soft croaking speech of the six-limbed race.

Even as he spoke the keen audio receptors of Jill were picking up the boom of surf.

The ship's boat pulled away from the gray sanded beach and they were left alone. They took up their swords and headed inland.

Brett looked across at Jill, since Kathryn now controlled the feminine super mech.

"Nice sendoff by the captain," he said. "But I'd trade all these swords and carving tools for one good rocket rifle."

"We'll have use for them, Ralph. That agan jungle ahead is really rugged. Have to hack our way through."

"That's a fact," Brett agreed, as his eyes tried to probe through the eternal fog to the top of the matted agan stems and roots, a living cliff, paralleling the shoreline.

The impenetrable wall must have reared hundreds of feet without a break. After having followed along its base for perhaps a mile, they were growing discouraged. It seemed the agan would never end.

It was then that they came upon the fresh muddy flood of a small river sweeping from beneath the agan's fleshy barrier.

"This is it, Kathy!" Brett cried. "We'll walk upstream, and eventually we'll get out of this jungle."

Jill's shoulders shrugged gracefully. She grinned.

"What have we got to lose? Of course there are any number of snake-dragons and six-legged lizards prowling around in there, and it may be a hundred miles before we reach the barrier cliffs above. But we'll have fun while it lasts."

"I'll lead off, Kathy. Save your belt light in case mine goes bad— and keep that sword ready."

"Better pass back a cord, Ralph, in case you drop into a deep pocket—or I do."

"Right you are."

They headed upstream. The bed of the little river was ribbed and matted with agan roots, and at first the water was over their heads but after a mile or more they were wading along a chest-high sluggish stream.

It was a dank echoing labyrinth of watery passages beneath the massed agan vines, and the faint current against which they traveled was their only guide. They heard faint distant splashing and the soggy thump of mighty feet and brushing scaly hide upon the huge roots walling the inky cavern-pools.

"A *sliran?*" asked the girl.

"I don't think so. From what Tarv Gan told us I'd say it's more likely a *drog*. An aquatic dragon would have feet, but a snake creature would wriggle or swim."

"I hope we don't tangle with them," Kathryn said fervently. "Even a super mech would come out second best with a hundred-foot lizard."

Brett grunted assent, and started on.

And then something long and rough and ropy flung itself around his lower limbs and drew him swiftly toward the root-festooned entrance to a side cavern.

Desperately he hacked at the sinister object. The sword bent back upon its hilt with the second mighty blow, the bronze blade too soft to penetrate the tough scales.

Swiftly he straightened the blade and thrust its point again and again into the barrel-thick pseudopod. He found a weak place in the armor—and then another. Jill's sword was probing and jabbing beside his.

The tentacle tightened spasmodically, throwing him to the bottom of the stream, and then it vanished into the darkness.

Jack came to his feet and took Jill's free hand. Wordlessly, they scrambled away from the monster's den.

After that they advanced six or seven miles, crossing one broad shallow lake, with supporting islands of agan roots dotting its sullen expanse, and circling a second, until they reached a series of shallow rocky cascades.

The agan masses overhead were thinning. They continued the ascent along a misty ravine-like channel. Soon they left the stream and used the blue-veined stems and roots for a ladder. Then, unexpectedly, their heads emerged into bright sunlight.

Kathryn grasped both of Jack's ears and pulled his head down.

"You know, if you weren't just a robot I could kiss you!"

Brett's heart, back on the sleeping plate inside the *Mallory*, was beating violently, as he said, "Well, don't forget you're only a robot yourself."

"Touche!" she laughed. "But just wait until we get back to the island!"

"I wish you'd stop trying to bring out the wolf in me, Kathy. One of these times I'm going to forget all about Waldo."

"Oh, darn Waldo! I can see I've got to tell you the truth. Waldo is my older brother. After he secured passage home for me on the *Mallory*, he started worrying. One girl alone with three men—and all of that … But if I were married—and to a company exec, I'd be perfectly safe.

"So here I am. And you can bet that after *we* are married I'll never worry about the female passengers warping *you* in. I tried."

"And who," asked Brett, while the two super mechs smiled foolishly at one another, "said anything about marriage?"

"Oh, I made up my mind about that the day we left Ganymede," Kathryn said placidly, "and when a Train makes up her mind …"

They had climbed the last four hundred feet to the rim of the broad Lower Plateau of Thrane's uplands. Before them stretched a vast band of luxuriant tropical growth, which extended inward for sixty or seventy miles to where a mile-high cliff, green with the bursting life of tropical climes, lifted sheerly. Above that cliff a second hundred-mile-wide shelf of more temperate growth stretched—and it was there that they hoped to find the descendants of the Americans who had colonized Thrane.

They had proved the reality of that mythical parallel world now. The six-limbed natives called it Thrane, and Tarv Gan had spoken of the gateways that brought ruin to his world many years before. So, once they had crossed the plateau ahead and scaled the mile-high barrier cliffs, they were convinced that they would see New Britain, Arrowhead Lake, and the busy little towns rimming its clear waters.

"Rough going, Kathy," said Brett soberly.

Swampland and moss-hung forest alternated. And among the trees they could see awkward, bony-plated monsters that made Brett think of the colored plates of vanished dinosaurs he had studied as a boy.

Overhead three leathery-winged monsters, with strange peaked heads and trailing legs, swooped and dipped.

He looked up—up past the Green Cliffs and the Red Cliffs above them to the Snowy Mountains. They stretched, like cottony clouds, along the southern horizon.

Over all, from an intensely blue clear sky, the three suns of this alien universe glowed redly.

"Ralph!" Kathryn suddenly cried. "Over there!"

His eyes followed her pointing finger. Beyond a bushy-tufted clump of trees, at the base of a low grassy hill about half a mile to the west, rested a triangular dark shape.

"The skimmer!" she cried.

The super mechs raced across the intervening reedy lowlands recklessly. Only after Jill had toppled into a quaking pool of slime and Brett had spent ten minutes fishing her out again, did they slow their mad pace.

Both Mercier and Strang were inside the skimmer, in a drunken stupor on the cushioned oval deck. Their raucous breathing rasped at the super mechs' receptors most unpleasantly. But Brett was grinning.

"Talk about luck!" he exclaimed, as he took their weapons and tied their hands behind their backs.

"Now what?"

"We'll drop them off on the middle plateau, up where the climate is temperate, and they can fend for themselves."

"And then?"

"To Arrowhead Lake or the Shallow Sea, where the settlements are. Then we'll be able to get that marriage license."

"And after that?"

"We have the *Mallory*. We'll recondition and refuel her. Blast off for some of these nearby unexplored planets—an entire new system to map."

"Like the Twenty-First Century all over again," cried Kathryn. "What a wonderful honeymoon ... But for now, let's deliver our prize packages and park the skimmer again. I crave a glass of stym and a smoke back on the ship."

"Can do." He chuckled. "To say nothing of a few of those kisses you've been threatening me with …"

The skimmer jetted cleanly upward and headed toward the Snowy Mountains and the cities in their shadow.

Stalemate

The bullet slapped rotted leaves and dirt into Gram Treb's eyes. He wormed backward to the bole of a small tree.

"Missed!" he shouted. He used English, the second tongue of them both. "Throw away your carbine and use rocks."

"You tasted it anyhow," Harl Neilson's shrill young voice cried. "How was the sample?"

"That leaves you two cartridges," taunted Treb. "Or is it only one?"

The sixth sense that had brought him safely through two of these bloody war duels here in space made him fling his body to the left. He rolled over once and lay huddled in a shallow depression. He knew all the tiny hollows and ridges—they were his insurance on this mile-wide island high above Earth.

Something thudded into the tree roots behind him. He hugged the ground, body flattened. His breath eased raggedly outward, and caught. The waiting—the seconds that became hours! If the grenade rolled after him, down the slope into his shelter, he was finished.

There was nothing he could do. His palms oozed sweat …

The grenade exploded. It was like a fist slammed against his skull. He was numbed for a long instant. Then he checked.

Unharmed. The depression had saved his neck this time. He wanted to shout at Neilson, tell him he was down to a lone grenade, but that was poor strategy. Now he must withdraw, make Neilson think him injured or dead, and trap him in turn.

They were the last of the belligerents here within Earth Satellite. For two months, since what would be May on Earth, they had carried on this mad duel. Of the other eighteen who had started the war in November of the preceding year, only four had survived their wounds.

The United Nations' supervisory seconds had transported them to their homes in Andilia and Baryt ...

Treb wormed his way as noiselessly as possible into the undergrowth, sprawling at last in the shelter of an earthen mound thirty feet from the grenade's raw splash. He waited—and thought.

Memories can be unpleasant. He could see his comrades of the three battles as they had fallen, wounded or gray with death. Too many of them had he helped bury. He remembered the treasured photos.

The draining wound in his right forearm throbbed ...

The enemy dead, too. He had killed several of them—more than his share, he thought savagely. They too were young despite the ragged beards some of them cultivated.

Treb felt like an old man. And he *was* old. He was twenty-nine. He had a son also named Gram, a boy of five, and little Alse, who was two. Had little Alse's mother lived he would never have volunteered for this third United Nations' war duel.

He would have been with her in the mountain valley of Krekar working hard, and gradually erasing those other ugly episodes here on Earth Satellite One ...

Minutes crawled by, lumped together into hours. Birds sang in the trees so laboriously maintained here in the satellite's disk-shaped heart. And, a hundred feet overhead, where the true deck of the manmade island in space began, other birds nested in the girders.

An ant crawled over Treb's earth-stained hand and passed under his outstretched carbine's barrel.

There was a movement in the clustering trees off to his right. Neilson had circled and was coming in from an opposite angle. Treb thumbed off the safety and waited.

An earth-colored helmet, with a trace of long pale hair around its rim, came slowly into view. Could be a dummy, Neilson was clever at rigging them to draw fire. And he had exactly two cartridges. After that it would be his three grenades, his two-foot needle-knife, that doubled as a bayonet, and the steel bow he had contrived from a strip of spring steel.

He held his fire. The trees made grenade lobbing a touchy business. And his bow was back in one of the dozens of foxholes he had spotted in both the inner and outer rings of trees.

In the fantasy stories of adventure in space that he enjoyed reading, the hero could always whip up a weird paralysis ray, a deadly, invisible robot bullet, or an intelligent gaseous ally from the void would appear. And out of scrap glass, metal and his shoestrings he could contrive a solar-powered shell that stopped any missile, deadlier than a marshmallow, cold.

In actual life he was finding it difficult enough to contrive a primitive sort of bow, a knife-lashed spear, and snares for the increasingly wary rabbits. Lack of sleep and lack of food supplies were sapping his lanky body of the whiplash swiftness and wiry strength it once possessed. Nor was the week-old wound any aid to his dulled wits ...

The helmet advanced; he could almost see the twig-stuffed gray shirt's pockets, and he let his nostrils expand as he sucked in a steadying breath. Now, a yard behind the fake Andilian, he could see the moving shoulders and skull of Harl Neilson—or so his bloodshot eyes told him.

He squeezed the trigger. There was a subdued yip, and then a derisive jeer. Missed again—or had he?

"Sour rocketing, Grampaw," Neilson laughed. "Try again. And then I'm coming after you."

Only Neilson wouldn't. Unless he'd miscalculated the number of grenades, he wouldn't come charging at Treb. And he couldn't be sure of the number of cartridges Treb possessed. He was just talking to keep his nerve up.

Especially if he was wounded now. That sudden yip ...

It was night again, an artificial night as artificial as the central ten-acre pool of water, the ring of flowering green trees and grasses, and the final outer ring of forest trees. It was here that the two thousand UN employees and soldiers on Earth Satellite One normally took their recreation periods.

Only the supervised war-duels, that since 2069 had been the only bloodletting permitted between nations, could long keep a Terran from visiting the green meadows and trees of this lowest of the three levels.

"I'd give half that quarter million," Neilson groaned, across the darkness, "for a cigarette."

"You mean," corrected Gram Treb, "half your ten thousand."

"It's the winner's grant or nothing, Treb. I promised Jane I'd hand it to her. Then we'll marry."

"But not if you are the loser?"

"I wouldn't—she wouldn't—it's impossible to think of asking her to share poverty and disgrace."

"I'd hardly say that. We lost our first war here on the Satellite. Baryt was obligated to cede a thousand square miles to Tarrance. Most of my ten thousand paid off my family's debts.

"Yet I married. I married Nal who had nursed me back to health. And we were happy. Until the second war with Duristan. I wanted money for her—for the children—for my impoverished valley."

Treb broke off. He backed away several feet and shifted noiselessly to a new position. Every night, and sometimes in the artificial sunlight, they talked together. But they never forgot that they were sworn foes.

"So you won it didn't you?" From his voice Neilson had shifted closer and to the left.

"Sure. And I wish I were as poor as before. For Nal was kicked to death—by the horse I should have been using—while I fought here."

Neilson made a sympathetic sound. Treb felt his lips twitch into a thin crooked line. This is what it meant to be human. To feel sorrow for another man's misfortunes—and then kill him!

Sure, Neilson was a good sort. Only twenty-four and in love with a girl, a woman really, widow of a dead lunar explorer. And he was a clean-living sort, nothing dishonorable or hateful about him. They even honored the same God.

But tomorrow, or the next day, or a month from now, he would kill or wound Neilson. Unless, as might well happen, Neilson got to him first.

He pushed aside a thought that came more and more often of late. Why not surrender, or let Neilson capture him? He did not consider suicide—little Gram and Alse needed him—although he had not been thinking of them when he signed for this ugly miniature battle in space. His wife's death had been too vivid yet.

But, why not surrender? He had enough money. The valley people could struggle along without the machines and the dam he had hoped to grant them with victory. And Baryt could lose the island of Daafa to Andilia without crippling herself. The three hundred and fifty inhabitants could be transferred to the mainland.

Treb laughed silently, a laugh that cut off with a twinge of drawing ugly pain from his wounded forearm. He knew that he could no more surrender without a fight than he could command his breathing to stop forever. He was a man, and men cannot give up dishonorably …

"I'd like to see those two kids sometime, if you're still around, Treb," Neilson had moved again. His voice was lower but he was nearer.

"Stop around anytime, Harl." Treb moved a few feet deeper into a thicket. "We'll show you what real Baryt hospitality is."

"That's a promise, Treb."

Killing. That's what war was. So you had to kill. Or you volunteered to kill. But you didn't have to like it. All these little wars under UN supervision were needless—arbitration would serve as well. But the people, the leaders—someone—wanted blood. So ten or twelve or fifteen citizens of one nation fought an equal number of the other state's sons.

Doubtless it was an improvement over the mass bombings of innocent city dwellers, and the horror of atomic dusts and sprays. No overwhelming army could sweep, unchecked, over a helpless neighbor. It was fairer, too, for those involved. Equal numbers of men, guns, supplies. Wealth if your side won, and a fair sum if you lost.

The United Nations saw to that. After all the avenues to peaceful settlement had been explored and turned down they finally permitted bloodshed. Much against their better judgement, perhaps.

So he could destroy likeable young Andilians like Neilson.

"Why don't you send up a rocket?" Neilson kidded, his voice coming from a changed direction again. "So I can see you."

"Anything to oblige."

Neilson was circling out around, as though to drive him into a trap or trick him. They were getting back to the primitive now. Soon it would be knives, spears, and deadfalls.

"Come on over and I'll show you Jane's picture, Treb," invited Neilson. He laughed hoarsely. "If we weren't where we are, I'd mean that."

"I know. I feel that way myself sometimes. We've been here alone too long. Hate hasn't lasted."

"Why aren't you a wrongo, Treb?" The young voice was cracked and savage. "Why'd you have to tell me about—Gram and Alse?"

Treb was backing away again, cautiously. He scented a trap. No doubt Neilson's words were sincere, at the moment, but in a second's time he could change into a cold-blooded executioner. He knew. He had seen the gentlest of men suddenly turn killer ...

And then his foot struck a yielding branch and his aroused suspicion sent him lunging forward.

A heavy something fell with a sickening thud, brushing as it struck the sole of his disintegrating shoe. A cleverly rigged deadfall of small trees and rock, doubtless.

"You're slipping, Harl," he shouted.

But he could feel the sudden sweat damping his palms, and the muscles twitched unsteadily in his arms and across his stomach.

With morning he was half a mile away, in a foxhole less than sixty yards from the massive outer perimeter of the arena. Two of his snares had yielded a rabbit each, and so he was supplied for several days.

The foxhole had two entrances, both well concealed, and he had rigged elaborate warning devices should the vicinity be approached. So he was sleeping.

His dreams were unpleasant.

In his latest dream an extremely shapely and smiling young woman with dark hair was heaving a grenade into a pit where he lay bound and helpless. The grenade swelled until it became a spaceship heading directly toward the frail scout craft he piloted ...

And a tiny blob of dislodged mud from the dugout spatted his face. He sat up.

Another day to hunt or be hunted. Or to lie here and try to rest and make plans. There was slight possibility that Neilson could find him here.

He gnawed at the scantly fleshed ribs of the first rabbit, savoring the raw meaty smell and flavor. Hunger was his salt.

Now that they had lost contact with one another it might require several days to find Neilson. A wooded platter, a mile in diameter, can afford many hiding places for one creature hiding from another hunting beast.

It was time to set some of the traps he had been contriving.

There were the two nooses, attached to bent-down triggered young trees that could not be set until darkness fell again. The net, too, would need darkness to conceal the four rough pulleys, and the rocks that a tug on his rope would spill.

But the almost invisible nylon cords, set at ankle height across the paths, and the ugly little pits with their sharpened stakes set three feet below, could trip up a man and cripple him. He must put out several of those.

He had no wish to kill Neilson. If he could capture him, very good. He could go back to Andilia and perhaps his Jane would be glad to take him. If she did not—it was worth knowing how little she really cared, was it not?

So he would try to trap the younger man and save his life.

It would be difficult. The other man had grenades, a carbine and a keen needle-knife. Perhaps, before the end, he would be forced to kill after all. But regretfully.

Treb dumped the last of the *tsaftha* antibiotic into his wound and lay back for a few more hours of rest before going out to prepare the traps.

His head was not clear. And his eyes drew together from exhaustion.

Another night and another day, and it was night again.

His traps were set and ready. All through the day he had prowled the trees, watching for some sign of Neilson. He found he was muttering to himself, hungry for the sound of spoken words.

It was nervous work. His muscles were jumping in faint spastic explosions. Neilson could have been lying in ambush in any of a hundred leafy coverts, resting there and waiting …

He had covered less than two miles of inching, crawling paths, his eyes ever alert for deadfalls, pits and spear-traps that might flash across the way to impale him.

And he had caught no sight of Neilson.

Now it was night again. Time to check on his traps. The rabbit traps as well as the human traps.

He was approaching the net. And the awareness that this furtive game of hide-and-seek might go on for weeks oppressed him. He might lie here close by the net for days without sight of Neilson. They were too evenly matched—and Neilson was younger. It was Neilson's youth against his experience.

He found the thin rope of knotted nylon and plastic scraps that led to the four balanced rocks. One stout yank and the net would jerk upward four feet and tighten around its victim.

But, in the dim starlight from the small globes spotting the Satellite's ceiling, the path was an indistinct blur. A moving body's exact position … And at fifty feet …

He saw Neilson—it could only be Neilson.

Moving on hands and knees, he was, keeping low and to the side of the little-used trail—but within the width of the hand-patched net. And he moved slowly, probing before him with a stick or his needle-knife; Treb could not tell which.

Another two feet and he could trip the net. Neilson would be captured, alive, and the stalemate ended.

Now!

The net flung into the air, snapped tight about Neilson's thrashing body! He heard the pop of parting strands as Neilson slashed with his knife. And then he swung the butt of his carbine, twice, against the trapped man's skull.

Neilson went limp. It was finished. He could take his prisoner to the lock, summon the UN guards, and go home to the Krekar Hills. And an end to all blood-letting for him.

He set about binding tight the arms and legs of Neilson, and had barely completed his task when the prisoner groaned and struggled.

"So this is it, Treb?"

"Yes."

"You win again. And I—I lose everything."

"So?" Treb touched his pocket torch to a heap of shredded dry twigs. "What have you lost? Your health, your life? And will not the woman forget all else and love you?"

"Hah! She will laugh at me if I come near her. Defeated, and with a paltry ten thousand to offer. Better that I died than this."

"Perhaps you do not know this woman, Harl. If she is good, she will come to you."

The growing firelight was on Neilson's bearded face. And beneath his eyes something glistened and beaded. He laughed bitterly.

"She's not good, Treb, understand that. She's evil and money hungry, and ambitious. But she is beautiful and I love her. I'd sell my soul and my body to possess her.

"That's why I volunteered. With the winners' grant I would have money. Prestige. Honor. There would be a thousand new opportunities for a career. And Jane could not refuse me then."

"It is wrong, Harl Neilson, to so worship a woman. Like alcohol or Venerian fire pollen—it is unnatural."

"I know. I have tried to forget, to put her memory aside. But it is like a disease. An incurable disease. I must have Jane."

Treb threw more wood on the little fire and checked over the lashings about Neilson's body.

"I am going to look at my rabbit snares," he said, "and to spring the other traps. We will eat and sleep, and in the morning try to shave and look decent before going to the locks."

Neilson let his head sag between his shoulders, and said nothing. He was leaning against a tree, his arms lashed behind him and to it.

"There is one more thing, Harl, that I wish to discuss. It is about the Paul Hubble Foundation Award. Think about it."

Treb moved off into the darkness.

The sunlight from the overhead "suns" of the Satellite revealed a greatly changed Treb. He was shaved, his hair combed and hacked off above his ears, and he was stitching the last rough patch on his dark green trouser leg.

Now he donned the trousers and went over to the bound Andilian. He cut the ropes, his carbine ready.

"Get down to the lake," he ordered. "You'll find a razor, soap and an old shirt to dry yourself with."

Harl Neilson was chunky and fair-haired, with a healthy looking red-brown skin. His eyes were wide and darkly blue. Now the wide mouth under his shapeless nose twisted into a faint grin.

"I'll try to get away," he warned. "Aren't you afraid of that?"

"I have all the guns, grenades and needle-knives, Harl. I'll shoot you if you attempt escape, of course, but I hope you'll listen to what I propose first."

Neilson slowly stripped off his ragged tunic and trousers. There was the scar of a recent bullet's path across his right shoulder blade. It was crusted with blackened blood.

"I thought I heard you two days back, Harl," said Treb.

"Just a scratch." Neilson took up the soap and waded into the nearby lake. "Start talking, Treb."

"I told you to think about Paul Hubble's Award, Harl. He's the American industrialist who opposed violence in settling any issue."

"Sure. Heard about him in the lower grades. Fifty million dollars he sunk in his worthless Peace Foundation. What about it?"

"Hear me out. Did you like what we just went through? Your friends and comrades dying—my friends dead and wounded? And all to settle some territorial dispute or to wipe out some imagined slur.

"Would you like to prevent your kid, or mine, from having to face this again?"

"Stop sounding off, Treb, and say something." Neilson scrubbed vigorously. "Of course I would—if I ever had a kid, I mean."

"We could help, Harl. By calling off the duel and making peace right here. Of course there might be new balloting—even another battle between our countries. But we would crack the theory that victory means more than humanity."

Neilson snorted. He splashed water into his eyes and over his soapy beard and hair.

"And go home penniless? To have every friend and neighbor avoid us? What's eating you? You won. You'll get the quarter of a million."

"I want you to share equally. I want our two countries to know that friendship means more than glory."

"I don't get it. If neither side wins we get nothing."

"You forget about the Hubble Award. Two hundred thousand to each member of both sides, or their survivors, if they declare an armistice."

"I had forgotten. You'd give up fifty thousand so I could get the same two hundred thousand! You're a prince, Treb.

"But I couldn't do it. Jane would turn against me. The radio, the newswires, television and the magazines would crucify me—both of us."

"We'd ride it out. None of the participants in the twenty-two duels here in Satellite has had the courage to admit he hates war. In years to come our stand would be honored."

"It means losing Jane. I can't do it."

"You've lost her anyway, Harl, if she's the way you say. How about your three wounded buddies: Wasson, Clark, and Thomason? Badly cut up aren't they? Clark blind. Wasson with no arms.

"Couldn't they use the two hundred thousand?"

Neilson was coming ashore. A sudden resolve hardened his face, and his blue eyes were dark and angry. His jaw jutted through the sandy fairness of his draggled beard.

Treb felt his vitals knot at what he sensed in Neilson's expression. He'd gambled on the essential fairness and sympathy of the Andilian's character. But now …

"I'll do it," Neilson said tonelessly.

"I hope you'll never regret what you are doing, Harl."

"Aw, lock valves!" snarled Neilson. "Get ready to go while I finish shaving."

So that was the way it was to be. Treb turned wearily away. He went back through the screen of flowering shrubs and trees to where the coals of their fire turned gray.

The grenades and the three cartridges, his own and Neilson's, he buried in a hasty hole under a tree's sprawled roots. Afterward he tamped sod back into place and spread leaves.

His needle-knife he laid on the turf. From his pocket he took a long strip of cloth and some of the tough nylon cords from the net. Then he let his trousers drop about his ankles and set about anchoring the needle-knife securely to his upper leg.

When he had finished the keen blade projected a foot below his kneecap. And around it, carefully, he wound some of the cloth. He donned his battered trousers again. The concealed knife was well hidden, although it did impede the freedom of his stride.

Then he went down to rejoin Neilson.

Neilson was just finishing hacking at his hair with the short-bladed safety razor. He scowled at Treb, his eyes on the carbine that the man from Baryt yet carried.

"Not taking any chances, eh, Treb?"

"Just in case you change your mind, Harl."

"My friend—my very dear friend—Gram Treb!" Neilson laughed. "What trust—what a faith in human nature!"

"Yes, Harl. Your friend."

They left the lake behind, Neilson in advance. Directly ahead, beyond the outer ring of trees, the locks to the upper levels waited. They had less than a third of a mile to traverse.

The rusting shattered debris of a machine gun, with a spilled clutter of empty shell cases, lay just off the trail.

"Harok Dann died here," said Treb. Neilson did not turn.

"The big man, Manross, was killed by Dann's fire even as he threw the grenade," he added.

Treb was watching the broad-shouldered figure ahead.

"Shut it off, Treb, will you?" Neilson shouted, turning. "Isn't it tough enough without you yap-yapping all the way?"

Treb's lips thinned. The knife chafed his leg. Already he was limping slightly. But they had covered more than half the distance. Once they contacted the UN guards and were through the locks he could relax …

The circular outer face of the lock was before them. And the button that summoned the guards jutted redly from a shoulder-high recess. Neilson leaned against the lock, his narrowed eyes on Treb as he reached for the button.

Treb jabbed. And he relaxed inwardly. Too late now for Neilson to attempt overpowering him and claiming the victory. He had feared such an attempt—with the lust for the woman, Jane Vanne, driving him, Neilson might have gone back on his word.

It was tough going for the kid. But he wasn't losing anything worth keeping. And hundreds of fine young lads like him might be spared going through this ordeal in space. They'd …

Neilson's fist caught him behind the ear. That split-second of inattention was proving costly. Neilson clamped the carbine barrel, wrested it away from Treb. He raised it. Treb lifted his hands.

"So now it's me at the controls," Neilson said, grinning. "Any reason why I should go through with your Hubble Award idea?"

"The guards will be here in no more than a minute, Harl. Throw the gun away and we'll go through together."

Neilson's eyes were shining. He was seeing the crowds waving crazy welcome as his spaceship grounded. He was seeing the adulation of the boys, and the adoring glance of the dark-eyed girl named Jane. He was seeing the medals and the banquets and the bundles of money.

"You were crazy, Treb," he said, "to ever trust me. In war promises mean nothing. Study your history."

Treb squared his shoulders, his hands came down.

"If that's the way it is," he said, and then, "coming at you, Neilson."

Neilson flinched. It was the first time Treb had called him by his last name, perhaps that was the reason. Or it could have been the sight of an unarmed man walking directly into his carbine's ugly muzzle.

He pressed the trigger. The unloaded weapon was silent. Treb wrenched at the gun. Neilson kicked him in the crotch. The gun came free. He brought it down at Treb's head, but at the last second before impact Treb dodged. The barrel smacked into Treb's right shoulder and broke the collarbone.

Treb came on, his left hand jabbing, and his right arm dangling. Neilson chopped at his face with the vertically held carbine, and tore a great chunk from his left cheek.

And then Treb's knee came up. The shielded razor-sharp blade sliced through his trouser. He drove the ugly little dagger into Neilson's body.

Neilson went down, squirming away from the sudden pain that tore at his vitals. The carbine went clattering.

Treb knelt beside him; tried to staunch the warm gush of red life, and cursed, soundlessly, the ambition that is mankind's greatest boon—and curse. He tore off the bloody knife.

"You won't die, Neilson," he said gravely. "Not with the surgeon and the hospital here on Earth Satellite so near. You'll live to see Andilia again.

"And about the invitation to visit us—I'm sorry you rejected it like this. But the offer still stands. When I can call you Harl again, when you are a *man*, visit us."

The lock behind them creaked and started to open.

The Pioneers

Gradually he became aware of resilient rubber and plastic supporting him. He lay on his back, heels together and toes lopped outward, elbows crowding uncomfortably into his ribs. His body shifted. The month-long hibernation was over.

A delicious feeling of completeness—of achievement—swept over him. He, Dorav Brink, had escaped from the endless boredom and idleness of Earth's mechanized domes, after all. Here on Sulle II there would be adventure and work in plenty.

His eyes opened. In the soft yellowish light which flooded the small square room, he saw a dozen other couches, similar to that on which he lay. Most of them were occupied. His gaze probed the huddled figures searching for the girl Rea.

He had met her aboard the space lighter en route to the interstellar liner that was to carry them to Sulle II. Then they had been given their preliminary capsules of *iberno* and he remembered no more.

Iberno hits some people that way—with others it takes five or six capsules to put them into the deathlike cataleptic state required for star hopping …

He saw her! Third couch to the right of his own. He stood up carefully, balancing on rubbery legs, and his hand went up to the constriction binding his skull. What was this? Goggles! Brink's fingers curled about the flexible band securing them. He tugged.

"Stop that, Brink!"

Brink's hand fell away. He recognized the voice of Len Daniels, the recruiter for this illegal voyage here to Sulle II.

"Want to lose your eyesight, Brink?" demanded the dapper little man. "We warned you of the danger. For at least ten days your eyes must remain protected."

The little gray-haired man wore no glasses, he had acquired an immunity to the sunlight of Sulle II from former voyages, but his naturally pink-and-white complexion was a sickly yellow.

Their voices roused the other colonists, and now Daniels moved among them, his soft full voice admonishing and sympathetic.

A coarse-haired giant of a man, dark hair graying at the temples of his ruddy outsize features, clamped Brink's fist with a huge hand.

"Name's Bryt Carby," he said, his voice ridiculously shrill.

"I'm Dorav Brink." His eyes slid toward the tall slenderness of Rea Smyt.

"Air don't taste much different from back home, Brink."

Brink made a wry face. "After breathing spacer air and being doped with iberno for months could we tell the difference?"

Carby laughed in agreement. "But Senior Daniels," and Brink wanted to grin at the respectful term used by the big, slow speaking man, "Senior Daniels says that Sulle II is like Earth in almost every respect."

"He would! And possibly it is. According to him even the animals resemble our own planet's."

"Once," and Carby grinned widely, "I ate a bit of cooked native meat. Ten credits it cost me. After that the protein packets and yeasteaks sickened me."

"I tried it once too, Carby, but it cost me fifteen credits. And that's the way Daniels and his company will get back the thousand credits we owe them for the trip." Brink laughed. "With food that we raise and meat that we kill, Carby. Daniels flies it to Earth and smuggles it into the domes as native to Earth. His profit must be enormous."

Carby frowned and rubbed a stubby finger across the bridge of his huge nose. And Brink edged away from his neighbor toward the slim tallness of Rea Smyt.

"Attention all of you!" Len Daniels had climbed atop a sturdy metal table.

"On the bulletin board just behind me the Commission has posted a list of your assignments and partners for the current year. Some of you will remain here in Low Park to work off your indebtedness, and others will be sent out to Middle Park and Devil's Elbow."

Something in the agent's tone, a touch of ironic amusement or arrogance, perhaps, angered Brink. But he kept his lips shut. In the ancient records that he had studied in the long idle years back there in York Dome, he had read of serfdom and slavery. He could afford to wait and learn if what he feared was true. After all, they were many light years from home and at Daniels' mercy—for the moment at least.

"After you have paired up and found the locations assigned you go to Warehouse Seven and draw your rations and tools. Your plastic tents will serve for shelter even in winter, but my advice to you is to build with logs."

The little man smiled a trifle grimly as he studied them.

"I would advise you to hunt game and raise crops as quickly as possible," he added. "Supplies and tools are expensive to freight out here to Sulle II. They will cost you five hundred more credits."

The colonists' faces paled and their eyes were sick. Brink smiled grimly as he watched. Well, they'd asked for it. Most of them were regretting their decision to abandon the ease and plenty of the giant domes already, but they had no choice now. Uncertainly they crowded about the bulletin board, and paired up as the directive indicated.

Brink found himself with a partner named Tzal Evans. She proved to be a genial, oversized, blonde giantess at least five years his senior. He had been hoping for a younger, more attractive companion— possibly dark-haired Rea Smyt. Yet he realized that the Commission could not permit its colonists to choose their jobs and partners at random. There was work to be done.

He found the map and learned that both he and Bryt Carby were assigned to the untamed, forested section named Middle Park. And Bryt Carby had drawn Rea Smyt as his partner.

Brink scrubbed at his chin. He foresaw difficulties ahead for Carby. The few moments that he had spent with Rea had acquainted him with her lightning changes of mood and her disdain for rules and regulations. Those two had nothing in common. After the legal year of partnership was ended neither of them would be likely to renew the agreement for another year.

Perhaps he, Brink, would draw her in next year's pool of unattached citizens, and then …

Tzal nudged at him. "Let's get our supplies," she said, her voice deep as a man's.

"Sure, Tzal." The top of her fair-haired skull was level with his eyes, and across it he caught a glimpse of Rea Smyt leading Carby from the reception center. "Sure. We better."

Rea danced along ahead of Carby like a child—a lovely slender child.

Dusk caught them, hours later, on the wooded ridge high above the broad valley that was their destination.

Carby followed Rea off the crumbled highway, that the vanished Sullans had built, and into a sheltered grove of long-leaved trees. Brink and Tzal, pushing easily together at the harnesses behind the rubber-tired cart, followed them.

Clumsily, for they had never seen a tent before, they released the forward section of the cart and drew out the slender jointed ribs of metal. They snapped these together into a low dome ten feet in diameter; and then Tzal controlled the extensible arms feeding out the plastic covering, while Brink locked the opaque skin into place.

Five minutes later, with the wind cone driving the generator and the bottled gas feeding the small stove, Tzal was preparing their evening meal under the soft glowing tubes.

She turned to Brink.

"Better go help Carby," she suggested, smiling. "That Rea—" And she shook her head.

Brink found Carby struggling doggedly with the metal ribs. His partner was not in sight, but they could hear her voice, singing softly somewhere out among the dusky trees. When at last the lighting tubes were glowing and Carby had lighted the stove, Brink eyed the weary, large-featured man curiously.

"What are you going to do about it?" he blurted. "You can't go on doing all the work. She needs a good—a good, lumping, I think the Ancients called it."

Carby grinned faintly.

"When she is ready," he said mildly, "she will help."

"Hah!" Brink snorted and went to the zippered entrance. "See you tomorrow, Bryt."

He crossed the near-darkness of the needle-strewn glade to his own tent. How bright were these stars and how sweet and cold was this raw air. In York Dome, with its thirty million citizens and its mild, conditioned atmosphere, one saw the stars only through telescreens or viewing ports.

Somewhere in the darkness a mournful wail, an aching ghost of a howl, sounded, and faded into the unfamiliar chirps, and hums of the night prowlers of the Sullan uplands ...

There was a choked scream from nearby and Brink heard the crashing progress of Rea Smyt toward her tent. The zippered entrance brightened and then dimmed as she shut it behind her. Brink shrugged. Stooping, he entered his own savory-smelling tent.

Tzal had covered the sleeping cots with the gay scarlet-and-blue blankets provided them, and their sliced and steaming rations were ready on the extended table shelf of the cart. Tzal smiled at him from the cot that doubled as a chair.

"Better eat before it gets cold," she invited, and helped herself to a serving of salmon-hued promine.

"Tomorrow," Brink said as he seated himself beside her, "we will dine on real meat—meat that I kill."

"Of course," Tzal agreed placidly.

Brink was remembering that easy promise, a month later, as he bound the last raggedly split stake atop the cabin roof. The cabin was but ten feet wide and twice as long, and built of smallish logs, but its cost in blistered flesh and exhaustion had been terrific ...

Six days had passed after their arrival here in Middle Park before his unfamiliar, lead-propelling rifle finally had brought down a small deerlike creature … the hunting wasn't easy—nothing here on Sulle II was easy.

He slid off the roof and down the trunk of a small tree that he had left here atop this grassy knoll. He straightened his hunched shoulders and heard the muscles grate and snap across the cartilage. He looked down over the grassy parkland, where a meandering stream watered the soil, and counted, for the hundredth time, the five young spotted ruminants that Carby, Tzal, and he had captured from a herd of wild creatures.

"Cows," Carby, and Tzal, his partner, called these giant cattlelike creatures, and he followed suit. It was easier to apply the familiar names to creatures that resembled those of Earth than to use the names supplied them at the Reception Center.

"Dorav!" He heard the voice and then the pressure of two rounded soft arms were around him.

"Rea!" he grunted, facing her. He pushed her arms aside, all too conscious of the shielded breast that brushed the back of his hand.

"Why are you here?" he demanded. "You have work at your cabin. The walls are only half finished."

The girl smiled at him. She was very attractive in a slim boyish sort of way. The palm of her sun-tanned hand, as she laid it upon his wrist, was not calloused as were Tzal's and his own.

"My partner and yours are cutting logs above us," she said. "We can be alone for several hours …"

Brink pushed her soft palm from his arm. For the past three weeks physical exhaustion and unwonted exercise had driven any desire for her from his thoughts. She was Carby's partner for a year—and Carby was his friend.

"Don't get me wrong, Dorav!" Her eyes flashed. They were blue and very dark and clear. "I want to go back to the Earth—to York Dome, to Sippi Dome or one of the other two domes in North America."

"I think we all do at times," Brink said coldly. "But it's not possible. Earth is forty or fifty light years away."

"I know a way." Rea Smyt's eyes were bright. "But I need a partner. Bryt won't go—he likes it here. And your blonde cow of a partner …"

"Tzal is okay," Brink said angrily. "Shut your mouth and go back to your own cabin before I—"

"We could go across the plains to the old ruins," Rea cried hastily, "and then journey down …"

Brink's work-roughened fingers spun her about facing toward Carby's cabin and the round gray tent beside it at the opposite end of the knoll.

Rea was sobbing angrily.

"I'll go by myself," she cried. "You fools can stay here and live like beasts—it's so simple if you only …"

Brink gave her a shove.

"If you worked as you should, you wouldn't find time to be discontented. And next year you can draw a new partner from the unattached pool."

The girl's eyes were hot as she turned and raced off along the path bisecting the knoll's green-swarded crown.

And Dorav Brink set to work building the huge stone-and-clay chimney that was to warm them in the winter ahead. The memory of Rea's words and the softness of her, kept intruding. Suddenly, he found himself longing for the comforts and the security of York Dome—he had been a peace guard, serving two hours every month—life had been soft and easy …

Savagely Brink swung his stone hammer, trying to smash his memories of mechanized, pleasant sloth as well as the harsh substance of the rocks.

It was another morning, the weeks of feverish planting and hunting for game to trade at the frozen locker plant at Center, were behind them. Now it was late summer on Sulle II, and even the early morning was uncomfortably warm.

Brink yawned and stretched luxuriously on his cot. Across the room Tzal still slept, her tousled, short-cropped hair faded by the sun, and her exposed firm flesh a ripe, golden-red. Her face was turned toward him and she was smiling faintly, as though at some pleasant dream fantasy.

Brink felt a pleasant lethargy. Tzal was a good partner, she never criticized without reason, and he trusted her judgment. His eyes ranged over the cabin. It was stout and well-joined—and their hands had erected it. Their credits at the locker plant were growing, despite the disappearance of most of the wild herds of "cattle." In another eight or ten years they would have repaid the passage advances and own a valuable property.

It was odd, he thought idly, that he never considered any woman other than Tzal as his partner when he thought of the future. Actually, of course she would request a change of partners, as he also intended to do, at the year's end. If the Commission allowed it she might even specify Bryt Carby—they worked well together in the fields and forest, and the three of them were good friends.

Suddenly he was aware of Carby's voice shouting somewhere outside. Brink pulled on his knee-length shorts and a sleeveless tunic, and struggled into his high, clumsily cobbled boots of "cowhide." He took down his repeating weapon and pocketed a handful of cartridges.

"What's it?" asked Tzal sleepily.

"I expect something is after the herd again," Brink told her as he went out the heavy, double-planked door.

He could hear Carby clearly now. He was calling for Rea. Brink swore under his breath and turned to reenter the cabin, but Carby had seen him and hailed him.

"Rea left in the night," the big man said. "She took one of the horses and a rifle. And she left a note. Says she is going back to live in one of the domes."

Brink whistled. The "horse" she had taken, actually a *ystan* according to the Commission, was only half-broken and a giant animal three times as large as its Earthly counterpart.

"The loneliness must have driven her insane," the big man cried. "We've got to follow her—get her to come back."

Carby's eyes were wild. He clamped Brink's right shoulder.

"Are you coming or not, Dorav? She needs us. We've got to find her."

The big man's eyes leaked tears. Brink realized, astounded, that the selfish, shallow, lazy woman—the woman, Rea Smyt—had won Carby's love.

"Of course, Bryt. I'll help you search."

"I will go too." Tzal's eyes were steady. "We must work together. When our child is born another woman will be needed."

Brink opened his mouth to object—closed it.

"Of course, but whether Rea is the one to …"

"She is a woman." Tzal smiled faintly and nodded.

"I'll follow her tracks, the ystan's tracks, westward across the park," Bryt Carby said impatiently. "She must head south or north to climb out of the valley. You, Tzal, go to the north end of the valley and pick up the trail—if it's there."

He shook the graying coarse hair out of his reddened eyes.

"You go south, Dorav. I'll meet up with you in a few hours if the trail leads in that direction. If neither of you find a trail and a day passes, I suggest that you return to the cabins."

"Best plan," Brink agreed. He called in to Tzal: "I'll saddle up."

"Right with you," his partner replied.

But, with the approach of night, Brink's big black ystan and his saddle-weary rider followed alone on the trail. Rea's partner had not overtaken Brink as he had promised.

The trail was clearcut and easy to follow—Rea was letting her mount race at top speed southward along the dirt crusted ancient highway. And Brink's half-tamed black stallion was endowed with stamina and speed that Carby's dun mare could never match … Now, darkness had blanked out the spoor.

At a miniature park's brush-screened entrance, Brink urged the weary ystan into the natural hedge of leafy growth. The big black beast snorted half-hearted protest and reared as branches clawed and stung him. When they were through they were in a broad grassy meadow, and in the fading light of a full moon jagged ruins stood etched against the darker trees.

He did not attempt any exploration until he had eaten of fire-warmed, greasy meat and portions of bread sopped in the frying pan.

Then he took a flaming branch, as thick through as his lower leg, and carried this rude torch into the ruins.

What had once been a street lay before him. Jumbled walls of brick and stone marked widely separated buildings.

In all, he counted no less than forty-five mounds, when he came across an isolated squared block of stone tilted at an awkward angle and half-buried. And cut into the stone was a blurred inscription.

The lettering was alien, yet somehow, achingly familiar. Brink dropped to his knees to clean away the concealing sod; but the spell of concentration was broken by a racing, swelling tattoo of hoofbeats. He sprang to his feet, remembering that he had left his rifle near the fire.

The rider could be Bryt Carby—or it could be some as yet undiscovered savage, native to the planet, or even Rea returning in panic.

He found his rifle, stepped through the rim of bushes beside the ancient highway and waited in their shadow. The indistinct bulk of a ystan grew larger in the pale light of Sulle II's lone satellite. At first Brink could see no rider; then he saw the huddled lump of darkness above the saddle. He stepped out into the road.

"Rea?" he said. His rifle lifted above the horizontal, its butt at his hip.

"Woa," the rider moaned faintly, and the trembling ystan came to a drooping stand.

Brink reached up to the rider to help her down.

"No," Rea whispered. "Hide me—hide—horse. Savages ..."

Brink grunted under his breath and tugged at the steaming ystan's bit to lead the beast off the highway. They pushed through the clawing branches, the ystan's breathing stentorian and ragged. The exhausted mount was dying on its feet.

They had scarcely reached the open meadow within, when the ystan collapsed. Rea fell with him, her right leg pinned under the twitching wet hulk. As Brink tugged her leg free, she groaned and went limp in his arms. Only then did he feel the stickiness of half-dried blood on her tunic and discover the sharp arrowhead that projected a full two inches from the front of her left shoulder blade.

Gently he whittled at the arrow's exposed shaft until the irregular metal head dropped off and then he jerked the arrow from the wound. He was glad that she was unconscious.

The distant voices of humans, shouting unintelligible phrases, warned him of the approach of the savages. The fire! With his hands he smothered and buried the flames. It was possible that the aborigines might pass them by. He could not banish the smell of smoke as he had the telltale glow of the coals, but the direction of the wind might protect them ...

The stiffening loom of the ystan lay between them and the park's brushy entrance. Carefully he slid his rifle up and over the saddle.

Voices and the sliding, chomp-tramp of hide-shod feet came and passed on. They had missed the break in the return tracks of Rea's ystan. Or, perhaps, the hoofprints of Brink's mount seemed to them a continuation of her spoor.

"I am awake," a small voice whispered beside him.

"Are you in pain, Rea?"

"Not much. Too near being dead for that. I'm done."

"No chance." Brink's voice was flat and false. She must have lost most of her blood. "How did it happen?"

"Was heading south on this highway. Planned to turn east soon. To Denver or some other deserted city where I might find a tube shuttle to Sippi Dome. You realize—this is really Earth?"

"Just now," Brink agreed gruffly. "Found a cornerstone. Must have been a public building—a bank they called it. This was Collrada Nation, or State."

"I knew ... weeks ago. Tried to tell you. So ... started alone."

She sat up suddenly, as though propelled by springs, and her good arm motioned toward the moonlit heights. She tried to say something, choked, and fell back.

There was no pulse ...

The third day after Rea's death. Three days, and three of the hairy, half-naked white savages, he thought grimly. He had never killed a fellow being before—in York Dome hatred and love and loyalty were

106

mere words from the barbarian centuries—but now he had destroyed three of his own kind. Nor did he feel any shame or regret …

The savages on Rea's backtrail had come upon Bryt Carby. He had killed one of them before they had overpowered him and built their fires.

Carby had not died until an hour after Brink had come upon the howling pack of six warriors and had emptied his gun into them. He had killed two of them outright and wounded three others; and then he had cared for the broken, blistered thing that had been his friend, until Carby died.

Now he watched before the cave where two savages lay hidden— and he watched the growing swarmings of green-bodied flies about the elevated rocky lip of their shelter.

The warriors must not escape to carry word back to their tribesmen of the settlement of the men from York Dome …

At a sound from behind him, he turned about, his rifle butt dug into his shoulder and chest, his finger pressing the firing button.

"Tzal!"

Behind the boulder overlooking the savages' rocky death trap he took her in his arms. She was Tzal, smiling and full-bodied as always, and his partner for this year and for the other years. The years yet to come.

She was dirt-streaked and sweaty. Her clothes were torn and her hair was matted and discolored with dust. Weariness darkened the skin beneath her eyes … She was beautiful!

"Where," she asked him after a time, "are they hidden?"

"Up there, just back of those—"

He spun about, racing back to where he had dropped his rifle. The two savages, wounded and limping grotesquely, were scuttling toward a broken jumble of rock fragments. Once hidden there they might work up the slope and escape.

Tzal's rifle cracked, once, twice, even as he turned and brought up his own weapon. A defiant yell slapped across the rocky slot and an arrow thudded weakly at Tzal's feet. Brink's thumb hit the firing button and the warrior spun about and fell across the man Tzal had shot.

For now the settlements were safe. The colonists, bargaining years of hard work for a supposed passage to a distant unsettled world, were secure from attack. Only a few hours from their luxurious home domes, they could sweat and toil and suffer as the hardy explorers of the earlier centuries must have done.

Dorav Brink wanted to laugh—to tell Tzal and the others of the colossal duping they had experienced. Yet he kept silent. From the evil of the trickery a great good might come. For the first time in centuries men were living an active, brain-stimulating life.

Let the great hothouse domes with their dwarfish inbred animals in their parks, and their controlled atmosphere, and odor content index, and mass-produced pleasure booths go their way. Let the pale, thready-muscled humans nibble their synthetic promines and yeasteaks—the pioneers had no need for substitutes ...

Brink's arm went around Tzal's shoulders and he was looking into her shaken, tear-stained eyes. He smiled. It was the first time he had ever seen his placid partner so moved.

"All this," Brink said, his hand sweeping, "for our son, and for the sons to follow him. Our children will make of Sulle II a better world than Earth."

Tzal's lips trembled. She had not heard him, he thought. His head lifted yet higher and he filled his lungs with the crisp upland air. Tzal was clinging to him, depending on him ...

Precisely, perhaps, as Tzal wished him to feel.

Memorium

"Tell me about Gramr, Granthr," the thin-faced little boy demanded. "You promised to tell me about my three Gramrs."

Vance Norall's attention snapped reluctantly back to his visitor. It was perhaps not surprising that he should have dropped off for a moment. At a hundred and thirty such a lapse was understandable … His eyes cleared.

"Ah, yes. Your great, great grandmothers, Ronnie. First of all there was Elsie. A lovely woman. Tall she was—taller than I, and dark. She rode well, swam well—even played championship golf. There was nothing she could not do."

Including lying, his mind wanted to add. After her death, when in a fit of anger she had driven too fast and crashed into a nest of highway posts, her memorium tapes had been brought to him in the hospital where he was recuperating. And from the tapes he learned what he had never really suspected—that her affections were as unstable and as unpredictable as her golf game was accurate.

She had loved him. The tapes, at five-year intervals, had confirmed that. But in the fifteen years of their life together she had had many regrettable episodes to recall—times when anger or loneliness had driven her to seek other companions.

"We were happy, Ronnie. I was teaching in an upstate college and your Gramr Elsie was touring the world collecting trophies. I remember seeing her on television talking with kings, prime ministers and presidents …"

It had been a miserable, lonely life for Elsie. The tapes told the real truth of those years. Her gay letters home had been mainly untruths. Yet a hard core of ambition, of a hunger for adulation, had driven her on. His first hurt anger at what her memories had revealed had changed to sympathy and pity as he came to understand her better.

While the second boy, Arthur, was being born he had resigned from his instructor's position and gone into business. And Arthur's birth had left Elsie in poor health. Her globetrotting days as an athlete and a golfer ended. And in rebellion she had struck back at him blindly and secretly—childishly.

The last wild ride that had taken her life, had almost cost him his own, and the will to suicide had colored all of her thinking in the last long period before that tragic event.

"Of course, Ronny, Gramr Elsie remained at home after your great granthr was born. And after she was killed in an automobile crash all her trophies were put into a case at the Country Club."

"And after that you married Gramr Vivian, and became very wealthy, and you built this living dome here in Antarctica near the mines." Ronnie smiled gravely. "That part I know very well."

Yes, that part Ronnie knew very well. But Ronnie had not known the austere efficient nurse, his second wife, who had cared for him after the accident. She had been a dutiful and thoughtful wife—a perfect mother to Elsie's two sons and their own three daughters—but always there had been a feeling of reserve between them. Even in their most intimate moments she had seemed self-sufficient and respectful.

Only after her death in her sleep, when he was sixty and Vivian was fifty, had he learned that she had a rheumatic heart, and should have slackened her headlong pace years before. And from her memory tapes, sent to him by the memorium proctors six months after the burial, he learned how distorted and cramped had been her philosophy of life.

She had hated and disliked all men—a silly, slightly sordid romance in her girlhood was her mental excuse for this attitude. Inwardly she shrank from any sign of affection, or any physical contact with him. Yet she desired marriage for the social status and monetary independence it afforded. Bitterly she had paid the price ...

"Gramr Vivian was an unusual woman," Norall told Ronnie, an ironical tone to his surprisingly strong old voice. "After she died I did not plan to remarry. I spent all my time in Antarctica building subterranean highways and developing mines ..."

"Until Gramr Eldris Arovvack," Ronnie rolled the *Arovvack* on his tongue, "came down to visit her son in one of your camps."

"I think you know all this better than I do, Ronnie," Norall said, laughing. "Maybe I should tell the proctors to destroy my memory tapes after I am gone. You will not need them."

"Oh, no, Granthr! It is against the law. Only after a hundred years without a withdrawal from the files can a memorium tape be destroyed. I wish to keep in touch with you—it will be like talking with you again."

"I see the proctors are doing a good job of indoctrination in the schools, Ronnie." Norall sighed. "When I was your age, back in 1950, the universal recordings of all citizens' memories was not even imagined.

"That came in the seventies. The Communists developed the system of brain stripping and recordings to weed out subversives and disloyal party members. They adapted it from our own process of clearing a disordered brain, in our mental institutions, and giving the individual a fresh start with a blank memory.

"By the Twenty-First Century all the major nations were keeping mental checks on their citizens, and eventually even the party leaders, much to their horror, were checked and removed from office."

"I know all that, Granthr," Ronnie cried impatiently. "We have it in school on ever so many *edutapes*. They say that the memorium is the greatest deterrent to crime and vicious thinking.

"But I want to hear about the olden times—when there were wars and singing commercials and big ugly cities."

"It was not so wonderful, Ronnie. Today is much nicer, and safer. When I was a boy we worshipped cowboys and pirates. Today it is the G.I. and the city gangster."

"Tell me about how you and Gramr Eldris Arovvack were caught in the vehicular subway for three days after that earthquake, Granthr."

"You know that by heart, Ronnie," Norall protested, "but if you insist ..."

Eldris Arovvack was in his mind's eye even as his voice went on speaking. Eldris, so slight, so daintily feminine and so girlishly blonde and beautiful despite her forty years and her grown engineering son. They had been trapped together for three days in a subway shuttle and he had fallen in love despite the twenty-five years between their ages.

For her, he had realized, this was a marriage of companionship and luxury. She had always known poverty. His two previous marriages had given him an insight into why women marry, but so deep was his love for Eldris that he wanted to be with her under any conditions.

And they had been happy. Despite the continual gnawing realization that only his money and position had drawn them together, Norall had enjoyed a long sixty-three years of life with Eldris.

She had died but two years before ...

"Granthr, I think I liked Gramr Eldris better than either of my other gramrs," Ronnie was saying. "Of course she's the only gramr I knew."

Norall squeezed the little boy's shoulder, hard.

It had been harder to accept the memorium tapes of Eldris than it had been to see her body disappear into the crematorium. For days he had refused to open the small sealed packets and insert the tapes into the reproducer. He felt that he could not endure to contact that beloved mind and feel there hatred, distaste and hidden foulness that humans too well know.

And when, in his great loneliness, he finally did renew contact with the recorded memories of Eldris, he was astounded—and humiliated.

For Eldris, through all the years of their marriage, had loved him. Her first marriage had ended in hatred, yes, and in pity for a weakling, but for Norall there was only a deepening respect and sincere affection.

And he had returned that love with a never-ending mistrust and cynical suspicion of her motives!

But he was happy now. After Ronnie left he would be alone again with her memorium tapes. Together they would relive the long happy years of their marriage. He would share her sadness as she felt that Norall did not care enough and he would feel her joy as their grandchildren, and *their* children, came to visit and to be married in the old family dome.

He must have been napping for the fraction of a second ...

"I must go now, Granthr. You are tired. Mother says I am not to tire you."

"Come again tomorrow. And Ronnie!" His bony arm reached out for the boy's bright blue tunic. "After I am gone and you are old enough to withdraw my tapes from the memorium library and contact them—"

He paused, his frail old fingers tightening on the fabric.

"Do not think too harshly of me and of your other granthrs and gramrs. When we were young we could not know that after death all our thoughts would be laid bare. Our parents and our nations did not know, and we were fed untruths that colored all our lives."

The little boy's thin face was puzzled.

"Run along," Norall said softly. "Some day you will understand."

He sent the wheelchair buzzing over toward the memorium tapes and the soft gray helmet for his head even as the door closed behind the boy.

Second Sight

His fingers moved over the modest packet of bills the invisible rockhound had handed to him. He smiled through the eternal night that was his own personal hell. Duggan's Hades.

"Thanks, Pete," he said gratefully. "Here, have a box of Conmos."

His sensitized fingers found the cigars, handed over a box, and he heard the nervous scuff of the other's shoes.

"This eight thousand means I can see again—for a while at least. Take 'em! It's little enough."

"Look, Duggan. I get eight hundred for selling you the ticket on the breakthrough time. Keep the cigars. You need the dough."

Feet pounded, thumping into swift inaudibility along the 10th Level's yielding walkway. His fingers caressed the crisp notes that his lucky guess on the 80th Level's tunnel juncture had won for him, plus the ten dollars, that this meager business could ill afford, it had cost to join the rockhounds' pool …

But now he was free. His own man. He was released from the calculated economies of his wife. Janith knew to within a few dollars what his newsstand on the 10th Level should make. He had never been able to save the necessary thousand dollar deposit, and ten dollars an hour, that a rented super mech cost. And she would never listen to his pleas that he must see again—if only for an hour.

"Waste ten or twenty dollars for nothing!" she would storm. "We have all your hospital bills to pay. I need new clothes. Your stock in the stands is too small."

What she left unspoken was the fact that she must secretly have hated his engineering career in the deep levels under Appalachia, and that she was dedicated to preventing his possible return …

After three years of blindness, under his wife's firm dominance, Duggan felt only hate for her. With this sudden fortune he could be independent. He could divorce her. He could rent a super mech—even return to work in the ever-deepening levels of Appalachia City!

First of all he must see again.

He closed up the news-and-cigar stand. With his cane's sensitive radar button pulsating beneath his fingers he hurried along the walkway toward the nearest super mech showroom. It was less than three blocks ...

"Be sure that all the contacts are against the skull and neck," the salesman was saying, his voice muffled by the *mentrol* hood covering Duggan's head and shoulders.

"Of course," Duggan's impatience made his voice shrill. "I've used mentrols before when inspecting cave-ins and such."

"Very well, sir." The man's voice was relieved. Probably he hated his job as much as Duggan hated his cigars and news.

Duggan tripped the switches and heard the building hum of power. An odd sort of vibration, that his mind told him was purely emotional, seemed to be permeating his whole body.

Abruptly the transition was complete. He was no longer lying on the padded bench beneath the mentrol hood. He was standing erect, conscious of the retaining clamps that held him upright.

He gulped a deep draught of air into the artificial lungs that did not need oxygen and his mechanical pulse quickened.

His eyes slitted open, drinking in by degrees the mirrored mentrol booth and the pallid, fat little man sitting beside his hooded body. He stepped out of the clamps, his sharpened senses aware of softness, and hardness, and scent, and color that human weakness so often blurs.

This super mech that was linked directly with his brain by twin mentrols was tall, chunky and gray of eye and hair. In a general way it was a duplicate of his own body, but there was no facial resemblance.

"How do you like it, sir?" The fat smile was empty, almost apologetic. "We have younger, more handsome models ..."

"Well enough." Duggan started donning the clothing that he had removed. "I'll want the mech for five, possibly ten, hours."

"I'll make out the slip for ten hours, sir. We'll refund any balance due you. But after ten hours …"

"I know. You must report the mech missing. But with my body here you can't lose."

The salesman smiled enigmatically. "We *have*," he said.

Duggan shrugged. He was impatient to be outside, feasting his starved vision on the stores and parks of the various upper levels. He might even take a lift to the Outside. It had been fifteen years ago, while their youngest son was a baby, that they had taken a weekend motor trip to the great scar that had been Manhattan. He remembered the vastness and the rawness of the uncontrolled atmosphere. It had been beautiful but also a bit terrifying. It was a ten years delayed honeymoon …

And now Merle was in the rocket corps and Janith and he were like strangers.

Duggan zippered shut his gray-checked jacket and left the booth. He walked slowly, savoring every picture of the crowded passenger strips beyond the walkway, and of the fairy spans of moving walkways crossing the travel strips. The soft glow of the Level's ceiling, fifty feet above, illuminated the double rows of apartment and storefronts.

It was good to see again.

Every twelfth section of the Level was a park. The greenery was fresher and brighter than he remembered; the tree boles and the branches were marvels of grace and strength. He strolled along the paths, impatient to be moving on, but aching with the emerald beauty around him …

He took the lifts to the upper levels. He rode the swiftest walkways and travel strips, his eyes drinking in the long-hidden sights. From an observation dome he looked out over the wooded mountain slopes of Outside, and saw the telltale ridging of rock and earth that marked the scores of hidden vehicular tubes linking Appalachia with its sister cities of Ondack and Smoky.

His five hours stretched into seven, and then, eight. Slowly a determination to keep these eyes, at whatever cost, was building within him. Always before he had agreed when Janith decided. He had been so dependent on her those first terrible weeks. But now, with this money from the breakthrough pool, he could rent a super mech—live as a man should live!

Duggan left the employment booth on the 20th Level, a badge on his jacket and a half-grin on his full super mech's lips.

On the records he was now Al Duggan, a second cousin from Montana. He knew that nothing in the world could bring Al further east than Ozarka. Just to be safe, however, he decided to drop Al a line to explain.

As far as his wife was concerned Merle Duggan was gone. Dead and buried. She could get a divorce if she wanted and marry that poddy, pink-skulled boss of hers at the advertising agency ...

"Five hundred a month," Duggan told himself. "Two-fifty for the rental, fifty for insurance—maybe fifty or so for spare parts—that leaves about a hundred and fifty for me."

He was starting at the bottom as a rock hog, a mucker, a clean-up man in the newly opened 80th Level. And his wages were the minimum union scale.

He took the lift down to the 79th Level, flashed his new badge at the guards, and took the gritty freight lift to the lowest level of the sprawling metropolis ...

"You Gaines Short?" he asked the lanky man bent over the littered desk in the rough plastic bubble that served as an office.

Sharp black eyes studied him—noted the bright new olive badge, and the creased, obviously new, coveralls.

"You're the new rock hog?"

"Yes, sir. Al Duggan."

"Any experience?"

"Montana—mining. Had some engineering. Worked in Ozarka on tunnels."

The lank man nodded, expressionless.

"You'll hog for a while. Later we'll see ... Any relation to the Duggan we lost a couple of years back?"

"We're cousins."

"Tough he couldn't see his way clear to try again." Short's lips thinned. "He may snap out of it yet … We could use a few more like him."

"I—I'll talk with him," promised Duggan.

He fought back the words that wanted to pour out. Whether it was a strange sense of loyalty to his wife, or a stubborn sort of pride, he could not bring himself to speak ill of her.

"A super mech is not so bad, Duggan." Short flexed a skinny arm. "I've worn this one since a rock slide crushed my back."

"Yes, sir," Duggan agreed.

Short scribbled on a form, handed it to Duggan.

"Take this down to Ted Rusche, he's the short, dark fellow bossing the rock hogs. He'll see you're issued your tools."

Duggan nodded and turned away.

In the Super Mech hostel, on the 79th Level, Duggan shared a compartment of six sleeping and mentrol plates. All of the others were rockhounds, and three of them worked in his own clean-up gang. His immediate pusher, Ted Rusche, was a legless, dark and hairy man, much like his working super mech. Waide and Myham, the first tall and once-handsome, and the latter, bony and scarred, were both paralytics.

Duggan's share of the attendants' salary amounted to another fifty dollars monthly. He was not growing too wealthy!

"And how do you like it after three weeks, Al?" Rusche demanded from where he balanced on the cushioned sleeping plate.

Duggan stretched cramped limbs and turned his sightless face toward Rusche's voice.

"Seems good to be working again, Ted," he said.

"This's your last day with us, Al. Orders from Short. He's transferring you. Office work, I guess, or maybe he's making you a foreman."

Rusche's voice was curious.

"He musta found out something about you, Al. S'funny but you look awful familiar to me too. And you know more about tunnels than you let on. How about leveling with a guy?"

118

"Not now." Duggan was thinking of the other listening men. "After we've cleaned-up and eaten. See you in the park outside the hostel."

"Right."

Duggan's thoughts were muddled. Fingerprints probably; at every super mech hostel all guests were printed and taped, and possibly through his similar name, Short must have been suspicious from the first. And if he had come to the hostel to see Duggan's mentrol-hooded face, while Duggan worked, his identification must have been sure.

Short knew that he was Merle Duggan, and before too long Janith, and all his friends—if he had any left now—would know he had been in hiding here.

He hurried to eat and get ready for another period under the mentrol's hooded probes.

Less than half an hour later he strode out of the hostel, his super mech gleaming and clean and his jacket and shorts newly pressed. He met Rusche in the park and they headed for the lift to the upper level.

En route to the 10th Level he explained.

"I thought you looked like somebody I should know." Rusche scrubbed at his pseudo beard's coarseness. "Accident left you sort of psychoed, huh? So you was scared of the Levels? Had to try coming back with a false name?"

Duggan gulped. It made a believable sort of yarn. He hadn't taken time to concoct a story ... Why not?

"Something like that. I guess I was badly shook, Ted."

"So now you go back to being engineer at a thousand or so, and I'm still a rock hog." Rusche shrugged. "Less headaches anyhow."

They stepped off the lift at the 10th Level and took the high speed strip toward the business section. Duggan had it in his mind to see Janith and tell her she had failed—that he was his own man again. She would be at the office. He would tell her off, and leave. And then he'd show Rusche some of the high spots of the low number levels of Appalachia.

The darkness came about them swiftly. To Duggan it was like a return to the nightmare of sightlessness. Under their feet the racing strip faltered and stalled. They were thrown off their feet and sprawled on the fiber-ribbed squares of the checkerboarded way's surface.

"What is it?" demanded Rusche.

He fought back the panic. This was not true blindness.

"Criminals. They set off a few dozen 'midnight' bombs and try to rob banks or stores. We get these attacks quite often."

"Last long?"

"Emergency ventilation will clear it out in a couple of minutes. And the Squads will have them in half an hour. They never get very far."

They sat close together, to wait. From the walkways and stalled strips shrieks and frightened cries sounded. The sounds seemed to increase from behind them.

"This's my first time above the Twentieth Level," Rusche confided. "Thirty-five years and I never saw the Outside. I don't think I like it up this high."

"It will be over in a little while, Ted. Probably just a group of teenagers looking for thrills." He laughed dryly. "They'll end up with blanked memories and new faces like those who tried before them."

"Listen," muttered Rusche.

In the lightlessness, and above the wailing of the terrified people about them, they could hear the scuff of running feet. They were coming closer at a swift pace. In a moment the runners would collide with them!

Duggan's years of blindness had given him the ability to judge and gauge distance from sound. At the proper instant he pounced, his hands clamping around a body, and a second body crashed into the leader. They went down in a tangle.

He heard Rusche shouting and fists battering and the tinkle of metal or crystal on metal. He was fighting desperately, his super mech's strength overtaxed. The unseen man's hands tore at his neck and shoulder, ripping away the synthetic flesh and baring the complex framework beneath.

Then his hand caught an arm and he exerted the full strength of his mech power, until now carefully subdued. The entire arm tore away from its shoulder. And yet the wounded man continued to attack.

It was only then that he realized this must be a super mech. The criminals must have stolen one or two super mechs and were using them in this robbery.

He was ruthless, then. He wrenched away the other arm. He battered at the unseen torso. The feet of the desperate mech smashed at his knees and thighs, staggering him. Then he bore the armless torso of the mech backward and fell upon it.

The mech went limp, its mentrols blanked by the distant criminal who controlled it.

Duggan came to his feet, listening for the sound of battle between Rusche and his captive. It came from his right, faintly. About ten feet distant, he judged it. And now the emergency vents were clearing the darkness from the travel strips. Twilight faded and vision replaced it.

Rusche was sitting astride a prone body, and even as Duggan reached his side the struggling criminal's arms and legs went limp. Rusche grunted and started to stand.

"A super mech!" he said. He rubbed thoughtfully at his disarranged nose and cheeks, smoothing them again into their normal contours. "What about yours?"

"The same."

"Here's their loot, anyhow," Rusche said, holding up a small gray plastine bag.

"Drop it, Ted. We better fade out of here before the Squads arrive, too. They might think we're—"

"Not on your life, Al. We should get a reward. Pics on the newswires and tapes."

Duggan shrugged and smoothed at his own neck and face. Four red-uniformed men, their heads hidden by ovoid gas helmets, came hissing toward them along the travel strip. They rode single-wheeled cycles and their rapid-fire *expoders* were trained on them.

"Careful now, Ted. Let me do the talking. They like to use paralysis needles and question later."

"But—"

"I've lived up here."

The unicycles braked to a halt.

"Step over here, slow," ordered one of the squadmen.

Duggan obeyed, careful to keep his arms rigid. Of course paralysis needles would cause this mech body no damage, but why make trouble? They *had* more destructive weapons.

"Ran into us," he said mildly. "We figured something wrong—honest men would be standing where they were. We stopped them."

The four members of the Squad were inspecting the damage.

"I guess you did," one of them said, admiringly. "You must be super mechs too?"

"That's right. I'm Duggan, Al—Merle Duggan, and this is my friend, Ted Rusche. We work on the 80th Level—rockhounds."

"Duggan?" The man's voice was suddenly strained. "Maybe you're not so clear as you pretend. A woman got in the way by accident, supposedly, of their getaway from the bank. Her name was Duggan too."

Duggan started forward, remembered the ugly expoder muzzles and backed away.

"Was her name Janith?" he demanded.

"Radio report didn't say. Contact them, Joe," he told one of the other faceless men.

"Couldn't be you hired these two to kill her and pretend the robbery?" he inquired.

"Of course not."

One of the Squad mumbled something. Duggan's interrogator dropped his weapon's muzzle.

"Woman twisted her ankle trying to get out of the way, and fell. Received a cut on her temple and is being taken to the hospital. Accidental all right."

"But her name."

"Janith."

Duggan felt a strange mingling of anger and of tenderness. The anger was directed toward the criminals.

"Could I go to her now? Rusche can fill you in on details."

"It's not—oh, all right. Regulations aren't too strict on these Levels. She your sister?"

"Wife." He turned to Rusche.

"See you at the lift in about an hour," he said and headed for the advertising agency where Janith was employed.

"We haven't been informed as to her whereabouts yet, Mr. Duggan," the receptionist at Duffey's offices said coldly.

Duggan glared down into the carefully pretty face, the solar lamp tan and the knife-smoothed wrinkles.

"Now see here, Blanche," he said, and spluttered impotently.

"See here yourself, Merle Duggan," the woman spat back sharply. "After all! You come running back just because she's hurt. Why didn't you come back like this a year ago?"

"I was with her a year ago."

"That wasn't you. You didn't have guts enough to rent a super mech and go back to your old job." The woman laughed. "Janith tried to insult and needle you into being a man again. And you just crawled."

"That's a lie," Duggan cried. "I begged her to let me go back. She wouldn't listen."

"That's what you say now. You don't want to remember. I know. I was here all the time. Many a time Janith has come to the office, crying, and told me how hopeless it seemed."

"You're—you're inventing all this, Blanche," he accused.

"I wish I were. Remember, Merle. Think. Be honest with yourself." Blanche put her nervous, blue-veined hand on his arm. A detached part of his brain noted how bony and brittle her hand was.

"She's loved you all these years, Merle." The tiny hand dug into his jacket sleeve. "To make you well again she risked losing your love—and she lost."

Blanche must be all of fifty, perhaps fifty-five, the analytical portion of his mind noted. Old maidish in many ways, despite her five ex-husbands; yet so sentimental—

"It's all part of her scheme. Pretend to be the patient, long-suffering wife and then secretly forbid me to go back to the deep levels again! You don't know!"

The woman's tired eyes sparkled green. Her little fist cracked against his chest. She turned half away from him.

"But I do know. I sat up with you many nights, while Janith got a few hours of rest. You were like a baby, slobbering and whimpering in your sleep. The days were worse. You were drunk and shouting and weeping. To you blindness was the end."

Merle gulped. He could remember nothing of the sort. Only the accident and awakening in the hospital to darkness … But there was a strange blankness, a hiatus in his memories, that ended with his hated job in the cigar stand. He could not recall his first day there or—

Could Blanche be telling the truth?

"You—spiteful old hag!" he shouted at her, and rushed out of the offices.

His feet pounded at the yielding softness of the walkway. The hospital was less than two blocks distant—no need to take a travel strip—and he needed the automatic motion of walking to steady his thoughts.

The forgotten months. Four months, or was it five months ago, he was in the news-and-cigar stand. That was the day when an old acquaintance from the lower levels sold him the chance on the 80th Level breakthrough.

That night he had begged Janith to let him rent a super mech. And she had scoffed at his wastefulness. Yet, now that he remembered it again, there had been a wistful note of hope in her voice.

Could she have been trying to fan his faint desire for sight into something more powerful and consuming—so he would become again the engineering Duggan he had been?

He had surrendered then, as he did many times afterward. Sullenly, yes, but he had surrendered. Perhaps she knew he was not ready for sight. When he refused to obey her, when he insisted on hiring a super mech—then, perhaps, she would know the cure was complete.

But that was only theory. He remembered her clearly expressed hatred for the mucking, lower-level life of a rockhound. Always his hatred for her grew as she spoke of his work …

She had never expressed herself in that way before the accident. She had gone with him on many exploratory trips into the caverns that the lower levels of Appalachia cut across. And she had enjoyed the experience—he was sure of that.

124

Remember! Think back. Back before the cigars and papers. Back to the days and months after the accident. It hurt to think. His temples, here on the mentrol-hooded sleeping plate, were pounding irregularly.

Huddling in a bed, knees drawn up and head tucked in, trying to gain somehow the safety that an infant once knew. Janith's voice, soft and understanding, and the acid of panic that set his lips to mumbling meaningless jargon ...

Why had Janith not sent him to the medical centers for mental clearing and re-education as was done with all cases of psychoed abnormals? The answer was with him. She loved him as he was, Merle Duggan—not as a new personality in her husband's body.

Artificially amnesia dissolves all marriage partnerships. She had not wanted that. Instead she had three years of hell.

Striking out at emptiness, his fists contacting soft flesh, and the pained cry, swiftly suppressed, of Janith. His voice, cursing and high pitched, as he fought the straps that now were restraining his sightless body. The bite of a needle and gradual dissolution of feeling ...

Memory was coming reluctantly back to Duggan. This was not the self-imagined visioning of an abused, helpless man. These memories were true. He had fought against all mental therapy and turned from those who loved him.

Now the hospital entrance was before him. He paused for a moment and then went inside. The automatic hush of the door shutting out the muted street sounds was all too familiar.

"Mrs. Janith Duggan," he told the crisply white woman at the desk.

"Room 212, second floor."

"Thank you."

He used the steps in preference to the lift. He needed more time to think—would he ever find enough time?

Undoubtedly, now, Janith's love for him was dead. His desertion of her must have finished the dissolution of their marriage. It had been cowardly—he should have faced her and declared what he was going to do and what she could do.

These past weeks, working with the rock hogs, had been invaluable. They had restored something of his self esteem.

The second floor. Pastel bare walls and soft voices. The odors. 208 and opposite, 209. A wheelchair, propelled by a timidly smiling white-haired woman. He nodded automatically.

210. What could he say to her? That he was sorry she was hurt and that he was such a fool? And then back to the super mech hostel and the five other cripples who shared the room?

212. The door ajar. A private room. He was glad of that. The headache was more violent now—there was a bitter taste in his mouth as his super mech entered the room.

She was alone, looking tiny and helpless on the high bed. To him, after three years, she was more beautiful than he remembered, even though the pure whiteness of her once-graying hair startled him.

"Janith," he said uncertainly.

She turned her head, curiosity in her expression, and then understanding came. There was no mistaking the warmth and welcome that came into her eyes. She held out her arms.

"Duggy," she commanded, "come here."

And he knew then, without ever being told, that his revolt and flight had all been part of the therapy, and Janith had known all the time where he had been …

Sole Survivor

The highways flowed northward, bumper to bumper, in one-way flight. Buses crowded with school children, and open trucks crammed with gray-faced adults, paced the mass evacuation ...

Shortly after Wednesday morning school sessions were abandoned, the cities cupping Wareton on the map had ceased to exist as units. Buffalo and Cleveland and Pittsburgh—especially Pittsburgh—lifted expanding, fiery fingers of death skyward. Shortly afterward the path of nuclear fallout became clear and all villages and smaller cities were warned. Headquarters had agreed that the Allegheny National Forest offered a haven.

11:45 A.M.
Erin Ward wriggled her slim nine-year-old body from its cramped nest behind the stacked dustiness of discarded desks and tables. She sneezed, the shadowy emptiness of the cavernous school basement echoing back the sound. She shivered. The unnatural silence was terrifying. She ran up the wide wooden steps to the ground floor and daylight.

Here the slow eddies of dust stirred by the frenzied feet of students and teachers alike were already settling. A hazy sunlight flooded through the winter-grimed windows highlighting the drifting motes. Books lay strewn about and little puddles of abandoned pencils, tablets, and treasured desk debris dotted the long wooden-floored hall.

The buses were long gone—Erin had heard the last motor fade, roaring, into silence almost fifteen minutes before. Now she could leave the school and walk two blocks to the railroad, cross it, and in three blocks more be home. Let the rest of them go. She had seen the Allegheny Forest and the river. Besides, they wouldn't let her tell her mother she was going and she might worry.

Of course her mother and father were in Cleveland, shopping, this being Wednesday and the barbershop closed all day. But Jeff or Kyra might have come home by now, what with all the schools closed for the day, and she could always go to Gramp and Gramm Ward's.

The big double doors were closed but not locked, and she had no difficulty opening them. A moment later she was skipping down the long winding walk to the street, her clothes blowing in the wind.

Wareton was strangely different. Even Erin's nine-year-old mind could sense it. She saw two cars, one of them on its side in the middle of the street, and both shattered and bent, but there was no crowd. Presently she saw other cars, empty, and parked at intervals along the curb, and the half-open doors of houses trailing strings of clothing and abandoned furniture out to the street.

Erin slowed her pace until she was walking, a great wonder and fear growing as she came to the railroad and crossed it. She had seen no life save two stray dogs that shied away from her, snarling.

12:30 P.M.

The pattern of the fallout was shifting. It curved, as the wind changed, the Buffalo fallout bearing northward along with that of Cleveland and Detroit. But now the Pittsburgh clouds came bumbling northward. Added to this were the secondary targets of Youngstown and Little Washington. These were now adding their fresh death to the seven expanded mushrooms slowly dissolving earthward.

On the charts along the Eastern seaboard it was patent that Wareton and its area had narrowly escaped one pattern of fallout only to be engulfed by another.

12:55 P.M.

Erin Ward was crying, the tears streaking the dust from the basement and twisted into whorls by her grimy little fists. She was heading westward out of Wareton along the highway, her goal the farm home of Aunt Ellen Belknap, nine miles distant.

Jeff and Kyra were not home, nor had her grandfather and grandmother been about. Back home she had turned on the radio and heard again and again the warning to clear out of Western Pennsylvania. Only, now, south-central Ohio was to be their goal.

Erin's Aunt Ellen lived in Ohio. Many times the preceding summer Fred and Celia Ward, her father and mother, had driven out to the farm on Sunday afternoons. It was only a few minutes' drive and she knew the way. So now she headed westward.

Just ahead was the blacktop road that twisted up over the hills toward the farm and Ohio.

2:05 P.M.

The cloud's low-groping fingers came up through the valley from the south and probed through the houses and business places of Wareton. It smothered the small barbershop of Fred Ward and flooded through the restaurant where Celia Ward and her sister, Myra, worked. Several score dogs and as many other household pets breathed in the lethal cloud and, all unknowing, were marked for death.

The cloud moved northward and now westward as the valley shifted. It pushed along the blacktop road and lapped over the low hill halfway up the valley's wall.

Fifty feet from its final crest a tiny, dark-haired girl in a red-and-white dotted dress clutched a half-empty box of rounded, brownish-yellow crackers more firmly to her breast and sat resting her weary feet beside the highway.

3:40 P.M.

She heard the car snoring through the unnatural stillness of the countryside, and quickly hid in a clump of roadside brush.

The pickup truck was red. Behind the two men in the front seat a third man was busily engaged in checking the apparatus in the truck's box. Their faces were grim and they wore shapeless, windowed coverings of plastic. To Erin's eyes they must have seemed alien enemies rather than the radiation experts they actually were.

The truck rolled slowly eastward and after it was out of sight Erin took up her seemingly endless trek in the opposite direction.

5:35 P.M.

With the slacking of the wind the death cloud expanded and sent out new pseudopods. One of these fingers crept up through a wooded ravine and wrapped itself around a halted pickup truck only to be thwarted by a clicking mechanism and the protective suits. The truck raced away, southward, into clear territory, once again.

Once again the cloud moved westward, but not so fast as the limping dusty figure in the red-and-white dotted dress. The blacktop road behind her, the small girl walked along a graveled road that stretched out smoothly across the last two miles that separated her from her goal.

8:05 P.M.

Erin came up over the low grassy bank of the roadside ditch to the long lawn's clipped softness. Twilight was not far away, and she felt a sudden emptiness as she realized that the Belknap car was gone from the garage. But she could wait until Aunt Ellen came back. Even if the front door was locked she knew about the concealed iron bar that was grooved into the cellar entrance.

The front door *was* locked. She hoisted the heavy cellar door, almost as heavy as her own body, and went down the cement steps into the cellar proper.

Erin hurried through the semidarkness to the kitchen steps and up into the kitchen. There were no lights, the power was off, but she knew where her Aunt Ellen's flashlights were kept.

After she had washed her face and hands and eaten she lay down on the couch in the living room and went to sleep, feeling confident that Aunt Ellen would soon return.

10:00 P.M.

With the strengthening of the south wind the area of contamination spread northward. The areas already "hot" were blocked off and awaited the decontamination squads. The residents whose homes were untouched were allowed to return to them, and with them they brought as many guests as they could accommodate. The valley where

Wareton lay was off limits and a solid area of contamination barred the Ohio border from the evacuees. And now, from the East, new clouds closed the trap.

Along the gravel road that was the only clean path into a large island of uncontaminated farmland drove the three cars bound for the Belknap farm. Ellen Belknap whispered a "Thank You, God" as they drove into the yard.

10:10 P.M.

"It's Erin!" She heard someone cry out, and someone was holding her too tightly.

She came awake and looked solemnly around at the strange faces. In the flickering yellow gleam of the kerosene lamps that the Belknaps had lighted she recognized no one. Not at first. And then she saw that Aunt Ellen held her, and Uncle Keith was there.

"Aren't Mother and Daddy with you?" she asked.

She saw Uncle Keith look at her aunt and turn his head.

"Maybe tomorrow," Aunt Ellen said softly. "Now it's time for bed."

Moment of Truth

She had been asleep. Now she stretched luxuriously beneath the crisp white sheet that the vapid August heat decreed. From memory to memory her dream-fogged mind drifted, and to the yet-to-be. It was good to remember, and to imagine, and to see and feel and hear ...

She smiled. She was Ruth Halsey, fourteen, brunette, and pretty. Earl, and Harry, and Buhl had told her she was pretty. Especially Buhl. Buhl was her favorite date now.

The room closed around her with its familiar colors and furnishings. Sometimes she would dream that she was elsewhere, unfamiliar, ugly places, but then she would awaken to the four long windows with their coarse beige drapes of monk's cloth and the fantasies were forever dispelled.

Her eyes loved the two paintings, the dark curls of the pink-and-white doll sitting prissily atop the dresser, and the full-length mirror on the open closet door.

The pictured design of the wallpaper, its background merging with the pastel blue of the slanted ceiling ... Almost as they had blended together that first day when she was twelve. Yet not the same, she corrected her thoughts, frowning. Sometimes, as today, the design seemed faded and changed. The gay little bridges and the flowered, impossibly blue trees seemed to change and threaten to vanish.

She laughed over at the demurely sitting doll. Essie had been her favorite doll when she was younger. Of course now that she was fourteen she did not play with dolls any more. But it was permissible that she keep her old friend neatly dressed and ever at hand as a confidant. She smiled at the thought. Essie never tattled.

"It must be from that polio," she told Essie, knowing all the time that she was almost well now and needed plenty of rest and careful doses of exercise. "It makes my eyes—funny."

Essie smiled back glassily and Ruth laughed. It was good to awaken and see the thick black arms of the maple tree outside the windows. It was good to have the cool green leaves waving at her, and see the filtered dapplings of sunshine cross and recross them.

She loved that old tree. She had played among its long horizontal branches from childhood. Her brother, Alex, who had been killed in the Normandy Landing during World War Third, had loved the tree too. He had built the railed, shingled-roofed little nest high up in the tree's crotched heart where Ruth kept some of her extra-special notes and jewelry and a book of poems.

One of the two paintings on the bedroom walls was of the old tree. The tree dominated the old story-and-a-half white house with the green shutters that was the Halsey's home. Her home. Alex had painted that picture as well as the other showing the graceful loop of the river and the roofs of the village of Thayer in the distance. Ruth had been with him as he painted that second picture from the jutting rock ledge five hundred feet above the river.

"I was just ten then, Essie," she chirped gaily. "I remember how afraid I was of the height and how Alex scolded."

But Alex was dead now and all she had to remember of him was the paintings and the photographs that Mother kept in a battered brown leather folder. For a moment the bright sunlight in her beloved maple tree's leaves seemed to dim and the room wavered about her. She wondered about that. She must tell her father or her mother.

Perhaps the polio, light touch of it or not, had hurt her eyesight. Glasses! She shuddered at the thought.

The room shimmered and blurred—and suddenly broke apart to reform into something … She squinched her eyes shut to the hideous vision. And then opened them the merest slit.

Nothing had changed …

"Mother!" she cried. "Daddy!" she cried. "What has happened?"

She heard the door to—to this hideous travesty of a room opening. Her eyes darted around the shrunken metal-walled shell, even the ceiling curved overhead, and she saw two grotesque daubs taped to the walls that parodied the paintings of her dead brother Alex. The coloring was ugly and the proportions out of line. And it was not canvas but curling sheets of paper taped and painted to resemble frames!

A big man, sandy-haired and with vertical wrinkles deep between piercing blue eyes, came into the room. She shrank into the bed, seeing that the sheet she tugged taut across her breast was ragged and blue.

"Ruth," he said, a slow smile making his face almost handsome, "you're better. You haven't spoken in weeks."

Ruth wanted to giggle. As though they could keep her quiet. Daddy was always shushing her … But who was this big man in his dusty drab coveralls and dropped dust mask dangling upon his chest?

"Don't you know me, dear? It's Buhl, your husband."

Buhl was fifteen and only a couple of inches taller than Ruth. Of course he had sandy hair like this man. But this man was old enough to be Buhl's father. This was crazy—like one of the dreams that always made her unhappy.

So? So it was a dream. She felt warmth and release. Why not see what this dream had to offer that might be amusing to remember and tell Buhl sometime soon? Wouldn't he laugh when he heard she had dreamed about him? And been married to him.

She saw the strip of shiny metal that masqueraded as her mirror, and where her four long windows, with their thick, loose-woven drapes, had been there were only four taped strips of paper with crude pictures of draped windows daubed on them. There were even green dabs of paint and black splashes to stimulate her beloved maple tree.

"Ruth! Do you feel better now? Please don't smile at me like that. I know you loved the baby, but this Martian atmosphere is tough even for men. It wasn't your fault."

"Go ahead and talk." Ruth laughed gaily. "This is just another bad dream and I know it. I'll wake up in a little while and be back in my cool old room."

"Blast your room and your dreams!"

The man went across the room in a swift rush and tore down one of the false windows, the painted strip of paper. And beyond, through a dusty oval glass window, Ruth could see a reddish brown wasteland, where dust clouds spun and shifted slowly, and a dusty huddle of what looked like Quonset huts or storage sheds of metal.

"That is reality, Ruth. You must face it. This pretense, this sleazy imitation of your old room is wrong. You're strong enough, and I love you—you can accept truth."

His face changed, all expression sponged from it in an instant as he looked into her eyes, and then it seemed to dissolve into something ugly and yet childish. She saw tears burst through and furrow the dust on his cheeks.

"Dear Lord," he cried, almost reverently, "must this go on forever? Will she ever come back to me?"

His voice choked off and he stumbled across the room and out the door. She heard it shut behind him, and she was hunting for Essie, already having forgotten the ill-mannered intruder.

There was no Essie, only a manikin of cloth-stuffed white nylon and lipstick, with black nylon for hair.

And then the room shimmered and broke apart and reformed and she was back in her bed with the sun on the slowly dancing green leaves outside the four long windows. Essie was smiling down at her from the dresser, and the paintings were as always, soft colors and perfectly drafted.

Had she thought there were four windows? How silly of her. The second from the right was a small oval of glass, or rather, a glass-covered picture of a desert scene. Odd that she had forgotten about that picture. Oh well, what did it matter?

In a few days she would be well enough again to climb out on the giant limbs and into the tree nest that her brother, Alex, had built. And the boys would come to see her and take her to the drugstore for sodas and sundaes.

Yes, she was sure now. She *did* like Buhl Austin best ...

Utility Girl

During the early years of star hopping, after the problem of multiple light speed was broken, and light years were covered in months or weeks, space crews often needed extra hands. Utility hands, or apprentices, were signed on with the understanding that death or injury to the regulars might allow them to become crewmen. By use of intensive edutapes, they could be trained in a matter of days for the specialized duties. Pay was microscopic, but the glamor of star hopping, plus chronic unemployment on overcrowded Terra, kept the pool of men and women ever full.

Aboard a passenger liner, a utility tour could be very pleasant and instructive. To this branch of space hopping, ambitious young citizens of Terra and Mars flocked. The freighter service was something else, again; only the despairing or apathetic signed up with it. Consequently, the utility berth on a freighter was often unfilled ...

The intercom grunted in the clipped Interling phrases of space, "Replacement Ute reporting aboard, sir. Wish to interview her?"

My jaws snapped. "Her? A woman this time, is it? No! Show her to her quarters and warn her. No drinking or drugs!"

"Will do." The soft Lasdian voice paused. "That all, sir?"

"If my wife comes aboard—inform me."

"Yes, sir."

Was there a note of amusement or distaste in the voicing of these Interling words? After the voyage just completed from Aantar to Luna, they could hold few illusions about my lush, lush of a wife. She drank often and heavily; she was addicted to the use of powdered *eduha* pods, a potent drug from Aantar. Yet, despite her excesses she was as shapely and fresh as the night when I first met her in a nightclub on one of the hothouse asteroids. Even after seven years of marriage, the very thought of her thrilled me.

Because of her, I had fired my old crew and taken out Aantarian registry for the *Khan*. My crew were alien humanoids—Lasdians and Aantarians. Only my fellow officer, Ralph Alpergen, of Terran ancestry via Mars, could speak our native tongue freely. And now Alpergen, astrogator and mate aboard the *Khan* since Aantar, was Grisa's latest conquest ... For three weeks she had not spoken to me; she was gone Earthside, probably with him.

No use firing Alpergen at this late date; a hurried replacement might prove even more obnoxious. And, much as I hated the way my wife trampled on my sense of decency, I knew that I would do nothing. I was too afraid of losing her forever.

Perhaps this new utility hand might win Alpergen's interest, and send Grisa back to me ... I scorned the thought. Grisa's sultry, auburn-haired beauty outshone that of any drab female volunteer from the sunken gutters of Appalachia City.

I went back to checking the carbons and cargo slips of the supplies destined for Sebal, lone watery planet of a lusty, distant young sun charted as Groff D-3, and for the desert world of Kelso. In seven hours we blasted off for an overhaul at the asteroids and Factory In The Sky. At Factory, we would have the minimum of repairs. A freighter—especially one now under Aantarian registry—rated only patchwork overhauls.

In seven hours, we would leave the lunar spacesite—to be gone for not less than seven years.

I wondered what Terra was really like. Grisa was due back from North America, where she had been born. I had never found time to accompany her there. Always there were cargoes and owners' representatives and petty red tape to slash through. I had been born in space thirty-four years before; my education came through spools of edutape and a single year at North Mars University, and Terra's vast underground cities could not be too much unlike the sunken lunar ports.

The *Khan* could blast off at any time now. The sooner the better. Cities or space stations seemed cramped and crowded after the vast freedom of space. The hours remaining would drag.

Cargo slips, storage manifests, union cargo thumpers' demands for overtime, demands for more economy from the other partners, and a fistful of charges from stores and hotels, Earthside ... A final check-off of the thousand and one minor items on requisition, and supposedly delivered—not the least of which was warfarin to tickle space rats' palates.

The intercom rattled. " 'Lo, Glen." The throaty, almost hoarse voice made my stomach knot. "I'm back."

"So I hear," I managed, trying to keep my voice toneless.

"Alla space kinks unjointed," Grisa said. "Wait'll you see the dresses'n gowns I bought." She laughed, a low broken gurgle like a pleased child's. "All's forgiven isn't it, Glen?"

I felt my teeth grate together and lock. But she knew. If she crooked her little finger or smiled ...

"I'll be in your cabin," she whispered. "Something lacy, and black, and cool ... In an hour, Glen?"

"All right, Grisa. Sure ... And this time we'll really stick together. Right?"

"No more wild orbits," Grisa's voice said creamily. "I promise."

Silence. I looked down at the thinning stack of reports and bills. Forty minutes should do for them.

Resolutely I pushed the pink and black and auburn image of my wife from my brain. I must finish this quickly, go to her, and then ready the ship for blast off. The blood sang and throbbed in my temples and pulsed in my throat. For the moment, I was the luckiest man on Luna.

"So that is what the hothouse asteroids are like."

The words were soft and not intended for any other ears than the speaker's. She was polishing the reddish-veined metal legs of the ship's chart room tables, and watching the visual plate that monitored our approach to Asteroid 714. She was plain-featured, eyes wide and gray, and her brown hair pulled back severely. In shapeless gray coveralls and a limp cap of the same color, she seemed but a masquerading child.

"Ah." I studied her. Three days out and this was my first glimpse of the new ute. "You're the utility hand?"

"Yes, Captain," she said, a faint dimple denting her tanned right cheek. "I am Theodora Ellson."

"Look plenty young," I grunted, chewing all the while on an unlighted cigar. They were always unlighted aboard a freighter. "Most of our female utes are middle-aged. Experienced hands."

"Oh I can learn, Captain, sir," she protested. "Tell me which edutapes to study. I'm sure I can carry out my duties satisfactorily."

She tucked a stray lock of hair back into the coiled mass at the nape of her neck, and I scowled. She sounded, and appeared, little like the usual worn flamers who signed aboard.

"Why'd you sign up, Ellson?" I demanded gruffly.

She blushed, her plain face momentarily averted. It was a beautiful bit of acting, I thought—probably done by holding her breath or some other studied tension. I felt disgust and anger.

"It's my fiancé. He's an engineer on Sebal. He was to send for me in eight years." Her tongue was running away with her words, so rapidly did she talk.

"But after five years, with no word—not that I could expect any until next year—I quit my job out in Utah and came to the Moon to work my way out to join him."

A pretty story! These women off the streets of Appalachia City's sunken levels all have them. And yet ... Her eyes were clear and bright with unshed tears—as though she feared I would censure her or put her out the airlock.

She could have heard the glamorous tales, or watched the vid-dramas that glorified the impossible romances of utes and wealthy passengers aboard the passenger space liners. The more sordid side of life for a female ute aboard a freighter is seldom widely publicized. If so, she was in for a shock.

"You can leave the *Khan* here among the hothouse asteroids, or at Factory In The Sky, Ellson," I said curtly. "Until then, you are relieved of any duties."

Tears came into the woman's wide-spaced eyes. Her hands spread wide, pleading. She was already on her knees where she had been working.

"Please," she begged. "Don't make me leave the ship. I must go on to Sebal!"

I shrugged and prepared to leave the cabin. I thought better of it, however, and jabbed a thumb at her. "Do you think any man will want to marry you after you've served three years as a ute aboard a freighter, Ellson?"

"Why not? The pay is low, but the edutapes will improve my mind and earning potential. Of course he will want to marry me."

I laughed harshly. "Then he cares greatly for you, or little for his own reputation. To marry a woman who has catered to the eight crewmen of a star freighter for three years, and to do it willingly." I shook my head. "Is he really that broadminded?"

Theodora Ellson's face grew white and twisted. Her eyes were dark with shock and disbelief. She stood up.

"You mean to say *that* is part of my duties?" She looked down, her pale skin flooding red. "All the crew ..."

"It's in the small print, Ellson."

"What sort of work could I find on—or rather in—the hollowed asteroids, Captain?" she asked breathlessly.

"Waitress or factory hand, if you are lucky. There is little choice. Unemployment is as bad here as on Terra and Mars."

Theodora Ellson's back straightened and her mouth thinned with resolution.

"Never!" she cried. "I am going on to Sebal. Three years—I can endure the three years of being a ute—and then if Medson Blaiter does not want me, I will find work for which I have trained."

"Uum," I said, rubbing a finger along my newly-shaven jaw.

"Only one thing," she asked uncertainly, "could you send me word, and permit darkness?" She paused, searching for words. "I could not work with them later, if I knew ..."

I studied her downcast face with a grim sort of amusement. Let her know the suffering of waiting for the inevitable as I had known it. She was a woman like Grisa—not the same, not naturally amoral or a drunkard, but yet a woman—and she would pay. I hated all the women of the galaxy.

Already I had caught Grisa slipping out of the quarters of Alpergen—and this but a day after her promise of no more wild orbits! I must have known, even while she promised, that she was completely without honor. Yet I could not give her up ...

"An unusual request, Ellson. But—yes. I will establish that procedure." I relented for a moment. "However, while we are at Factory why not try to find something more congenial?"

"Thank you, Captain," she said faintly, turning back to her polishing, "but my mind is made up. I stick."

I shrugged and left the chart room.

We had spent four Earthside-days in the null-gravity of Factory's vast hollow interior while repair crews went over the *Khan*. The five bulky Aantarians, and the three fragile-limbed Lasdians of my crew spent most of their time in the shops and entertainment sectors that share the inner shell of the spinning cylinder with the factories. There the pseudo gravity is close to one tenth that of Earth, lessening with each inner level until the three-mile length of the spaceship yards is practically zero.

Grisa and Alpergen had disappeared until just before takeoff, but Theodora Ellson had remained aboard to help me with the food supplies brought to us there from the hollowed crystalline asteroids—the Hothouse Asteroids. She had refused to visit the outer levels of the Factory but she did go with me to one of the sealed little worlds where hydroponics have brought green life and processing factories. But she had not applied there for work.

Now three space tugs had warped us out into open space, and we were in space drive—our first destination a year distant. A third of our cargo would be left on the desert planet of Kelso, and then it would be two years in space drive to Sebal.

"But what am I to do with my time?" Theodora Ellson, her final check of the supplies finished, demanded. "Is there any objection to my using the technical edutapes?"

"You could gamble or play Aantarian *tchank* as the crew does," I told her. We were in the ship's lounge, Grisa, Alpergen, and myself. "Or Alpergen could teach you astrogation."

Alpergen's graceful long body turned away from Grisa as his name was mentioned. He always moved smoothly, almost snakily, his dark eyes glittering. He studied the plain-faced ute in her ill-fitting gray coveralls. He laughed. "Why waste time on a moronic ute, when I can find something more interesting?"

He looked down at Grisa and they both laughed. My fists clenched. I saw pity and embarrassment in the girl's face and I hated that even more. But I was Captain; a fight would solve nothing—it even might drive Grisa away from me for good.

"Sure. Use the tapes, Ellson," I said shortly. "In three years you should learn how to build a spacer as well as navigate."

She left the lounge and I followed a few minutes later. Grisa and Alpergen were too engrossed in their drinking and their conversation to know that I had gone.

I prowled the ship, checking on the pile and on the cargo. A silvery-haired Lasdian, long-limbed and nimble-fingered, was on duty. In space, the Lasdians had proved their worth over we Terrestrians—they could withstand acceleration and extremes of temperature and gravity that would render us helpless. Only a lack of concentration kept Lasdians from becoming ship's officers; their minds were like quicksilver.

"The ship is clean," I commended him. "You have all done fine work, Anl."

Anl ducked his head, his enormous yellow eyes bright.

"It is ute who show us," he said, his narrow toothless mouth grinning. "Is good nest-keeper."

"Better than some we've had," I agreed, thinking of the surly male ute on the previous voyage. "Not so bossy."

The average ute—or even the average Terrestrian—considers all alien humanoids his inferiors; and this last one was an exaggerated example of his type. Eventually the Aantarians had refused to work with, or around him, and he had come to fear for his life. The bluemaned, golden-skinned giants are stolid, hardworking men, but even their good nature could not tolerate a man like Hallek.

"We like ute, Theo," Anl said. "Teach her our talk. Aantar talk too, maybe."

I walked on, to the repair mech's control cubicle, and seated myself there. It was too bad that Ellson was a woman. A man could be groomed to take Alpergen's place—this would be his last tour of duty aboard the *Khan*. But a woman—no!

The helmet, with its thousands of needle-like filaments, I fitted down over my skull and adjusted. I closed the switch.

The hum muted and I experienced the familiar transition from a frail human body into the plastic-and-alloy robot giant that was the ship's repair mech. Through the scientific magic of the mentrol unit, my brain could see, and hear, and feel through this mech body as though it were my own. Not for us the clumsy spacesuits, the radiation burns, and the threat of sterility that plagued the early planet hoppers!

I stepped out of the retaining clamps and proceeded directly to the locks leading to empty space. I had inspected the ship's interior; now it was time to examine the outer skin.

Ordinarily, this was a routine job assigned to one of the crewmen, but I enjoyed being away from the cramped ship's quarters for a time—even though it was by proxy. It was good to be alone.

The year-long hop to Kelso was much like any other voyage. The crewmen were on duty week-on, week-off—their off weeks spent in dreamless sleep if they so desired, a suspension of life induced by minute amounts of *iberno*. It was iberno that enabled the first slower-than-light ships to reach other solar systems—hops often lasted for several centuries, then. In fact our new starships were contacting systems where the original expeditions were not due to arrive for hundreds of years.

Alpergen and my wife took their iberno shots regularly, but I refused mine. There was a growing suspicion in my mind that I might never come out of suspended animation once I entered it. With booster shots I could be rendered helpless, and on a later hop my body could be *accidentally* destroyed. And my wife would inherit my percentage in the Aantarian registered ship—with Alpergen to captain it.

I had seen it in their eyes, a secret sort of impatience, every time I refused the shots.

Theodora Ellson, too, refused her iberno. She was busy with the edutapes and with her duties about the ship; gradually she took over most of Alpergen's work. Never had our records been so neat or so accurately documented. In one year, she learned more than many a seven-year graduate of Terra's universities.

It was easy to forget that she was a woman. She was not like Grisa—not shapely or feminine or provocative. With her shortly cut brown hair, and her bulky gray coveralls she resembled only an eager young man trying to learn about navigation and space.

She came to me often with questions that I could not readily answer; and as the long weeks passed I, too, used the dusty tapes to refresh my knowledge. We became friends, our loneliness a mutual bond. I learned about her background, an orphan at eight, raised by a dour uncle in a mining village in Utah, and about the whirlwind courtship by the restless young engineering graduate from Appalachia City.

"And so your Medson Blaiter took the five thousand units your uncle left you, back to Appalachia with him," I said.

"He was going to furnish an apartment and buy a used hopter with it," she said. She laid down the control mechanism she was repairing there in the shop. "But apartments were hard to find."

I teetered back on my heels against the repair mech clipped to the bulkhead, my eyes narrowed with thought.

"And then Blaiter joined a mining expedition for Sebal," I went on, "and left without letting you know in advance."

"He couldn't, Captain; he had to decide at once. There was no work on Terra, or even Mars. Mining is almost dead—mines worked out or low grade."

"I realise that, Theo," I said impatiently. "But leaving without contacting you—and with your five thousand ..."

"That is to be invested on Sebal," she said quickly, "for me. He says it will be ten times as much by the time he sends for me."

I snorted inaudibly. There was no question in my mind about her *ambitious* lover. He had taken this simple rural woman's money and spent it with no intention of sending for her. She was probably only one of many that he had romanced. His enlisting for a tour in the mines of Sebal had meant escape from possible prosecution by *them*. *They* would never receive a ticket to Sebal.

Only, Theodora Ellson had decided to do something about it; she was following him on her own. In one year she had advanced, mentally, to her age of twenty-four. Given two more years of edutapes and Medson Blaiter would be confronted by a capable young woman demanding not only his name, but also the five thousand solar units—plus interest—due her.

She was a determined woman. She let neither distance or moralistic scruples stand in her way. I felt a gleeful sort of sympathy for Medson Blaiter. He would be getting what was due him once Theodora Ellson took control.

"Investments have a way of going sour," I said. "Be sure you check the receipts and records if that happens."

Her screwdriver clicked into its magnetized socket above the bench and she turned to me. Her wide-set gray eyes were hot, and there was a smear of grease across her nose from cheek to cheek.

"You think he's a worthless scoundrel just as my boss back in Utah said, don't you?" she demanded sharply. She blinked, wetly, and turned her head. "I can't blame you, though. Sometimes I think so, too," she confessed.

"We could all three be wrong, of course," I said, "but even if you lose everything you're qualified for several jobs. Mech technician, astrogator, electronics tech, medical aide, pile super and a few dozen others."

"I am not sorry I left Utah," she said thoughtfully. "There must be some sort of ugliness about any position, I suppose. So far, I have nothing to complain about on this ship, Captain."

Suddenly her mood changed. Her back straightened and her chin came up. With her streaked face and worn coveralls, and with her hands defiantly on her hips she was most pathetically unfeminine.

"Tell me, Captain," she said, "am I so hopelessly ugly that no man would ever want me?"

I laughed. "Theo," I said, "you're worth a dozen of the other kind. You've got something besides oversized glands and a baby face. You've got brains."

"Fine—wonderful!" She stamped her foot on the deck. "But do you think any man would ever want to—to see me around year after year?"

"Of course. I mean it sincerely, girl. You'll meet someone on Sebal, or elsewhere, who'll be lucky enough to marry you."

She grinned and headed out of the shop with her repaired control mechanism. At the door she paused. "I don't believe a word of it," she admitted, "but it sounds real nice."

That was less than twenty hours before we snapped out of space drive and dropped on cushioning rocket blasts to the dusty gray world of Kelso.

The mines of Kelso are spotted along, and near, the thousand-mile length of Kelso's equatorial rift. In this vast gouge, varying from three to six miles in depth and fifteen miles in width, a series of small lakes and ponds provide vegetation and game animals. Whatever caused the rift—a glancing giant meteorite, a volcanic explosion, or a vast trapped bubble of gases—it alone made Kelso inhabitable.

We grounded on a mile-wide disc of an island—flat, grassless, and less than a hundred feet from the mainland ringing the lake's eighty miles of shoreline. A causeway of rocks and other debris linked us with the mainland, and already the eight-wheeled beetle-vans, sealed and air-conditioned against the thin air and dust of the upper levels, were growling slowly across it.

There were supplies for twenty different mines to be checked out and signed for and loaded. The Aantarians worked with speed and all their strength loading the vans, for I had promised them two days planet leave. And the Lasdians darted here and there, directing the van drivers and their helpers, but doing little actual work themselves. We drove ourselves for the five hours remaining of Kelso's short eight hours of sunlight, and an hour after the sudden moonless night fell, all cargo was unloaded.

The crew left for whatever dubious entertainment the bedraggled females from their distant home planets might afford, plus an oversupply of their native wines and other potent brews. I knew that the first week in space would see a sore and surly crew, but with a two-year jump in prospect I could not refuse them liberty. The ship was silent again, save for the occasional tunk-tunk of the tireless female ute's tools in the workshop.

My mate and Grisa, as usual, had left for the settlement, and I was sitting alone with my bitterness and loneliness. A wife who ignored me, a mate who despised and hated me, a crew of alien humanoids, and a homeless girl who would do anything for transportation to her worthless lover. The years ahead seemed bleaker and more useless, as I viewed them.

Half asleep though I was, sprawled in the broad padded seat in the ship's little lounge, I heard the soft shuffle of heelless scuffs along the corridor. That it was not Theo, the ute, I was positive; from the sounds in the workshop she was testing the ailing repair mech.

I watched through slitted eyes. It was Grisa, soft, full-breasted and seductive as ever, who came so silently from the corridor, with her right hand concealed at her side. And behind her, his usual insolent smile wiped away for the moment, peered the dark, snaky features of Alpergen.

"Sleeping, dear?" whispered Grisa softly.

I made no answer. Apparently my silence satisfied her. Now her hand came up, a gleaming hypodermic in it.

Iberno! I had no doubt about it now. And Alpergen was allowing Grisa to shoot the frozen death into my bloodstream. No! The sudden shock brought me clarity of mind. It was Grisa who controlled the two of us. It was her whim to destroy me and briefly install Alpergen in my place.

In that instant all my desire for her was wiped out.

The needle came down toward my sprawled leg, hesitated at the thickness of my soiled coveralls, and came up toward my bared forearm. And then I twisted away, pulled myself behind the seat. My left hand smashed the hypodermic holding arm downward, and it fell to the deck. Grisa's wet painted mouth gaped with a sudden cry. She tried to manufacture a bewitching smile in that brief instant, but there was nothing to draw from on so brief notice.

A gun crashed, and the wind of a slug cooled my left cheek. I saw Grisa's green eyes widen as a sliver of her ear lobe vanished, taking with it a gouge of her glistening red hair.

Without turning, I knew that this must be Alpergen. Now, at all costs, they must kill me. Somehow, later, it must appear to be an accident; now the important thing was to destroy me.

I dropped behind the seat, dragging Grisa down atop me. As a shield she was effective, being almost as broad as I; but her body could not arrest the passage of a heavy bullet should Alpergen decide to fire.

"No, Ralph," my wife gasped. "Too noisy. Use the needles."

Tiny needles tipped with paralyzing crystals would come spewing from the weapon Grisa named. One of them meant momentary helplessness—a dozen meant coma and death, unless I were treated at once.

I flung Grisa aside, deciding to make a dash for the corridor and weapons of my own while he changed his attack. I knew that one stitching sweep across our bodies would paralyze us both; *all* of the needles could not miss. And Grisa, desperate, clung to my hip pocket. I lunged toward the other door.

The pocket tore free and I staggered, only to resume my flight. But the needle gun was sewing; I heard its hum, and spun about and toward the weapon. It was too late to escape the room. My only hope now was to reach Alpergen.

I felt the slight sting of a needle along my skull and was going down. The paralysis was almost instantaneous.

This was how it was going to end, I told myself. I will be conscious, but helpless, while they decide my fate. Over the side, here or in space. And some story to cover with the crew.

We had all forgotten the ute. Not that one small woman, without any weapons save the tools in the shop, could do anything to save me; the logical thing for her to do would be to slip out silently and carry word to the authorities.

But Theodora Ellson realized that she had another weapon, and she used it.

I lay in such a way that I saw the doorway to the lounge behind Alpergen. Suddenly the repair mech—bulky and very humanoid in shape, despite the unrepaired section of pseudo-flesh over its right cheek—loomed there. Before its middle it held a section of hull plate as a shield. One hand gripped the plate and in the other was a heavy wrench.

The wrench came up. Grisa cried out. Alpergen sprang toward us even as the wrench fell, and fired his needle gun. In a moment he realized the futility of this and discarded it for his automatic. But the repair mech had followed.

Two bullets smashed into the heavy plate and ricocheted. The wrench swung, battered the gun from Alpergen's fingers, and then the repair mech hurled the plate flatwise against the mate's body. Alpergen went down, unconscious. And then the repair mech spun about and darted into the corridor.

I heard a shriek of rage and fear that cut off abruptly. Apparently Grisa had realized that Theo Ellson was controlling the giant robot, and she had tried to reach the control cubicle. But the ute had anticipated this.

The mech dragged a limp body, Grisa's, into the lounge and dropped it alongside Alpergen. Then it hunted out the automatic and the needle gun.

"You'll snap out of it in a few minutes, Captain," the rusty voice of the repair mech said. "Then you can call the police or do whatever you please."

I tried to answer but all I could do was stare my gratitude through watery unblinking eyes.

Only after ten minutes of helplessness did feeling return to my legs and arms, and finally to my torso. A measure of numbness remained but I could get about and speak. The mech handed me the weapons and stood waiting.

"Thanks, Theo," I said, staring down at the scheming pair. "As of now you are mate and astrogator. We'll pick up another ute."

"What about these two?"

"Alpergen gets off without arrest, and with his pay and equipment; a police investigation would keep us here for weeks."

"And—your wife?"

"I'm cured. She's just another space girl to me now. She goes planetside along with Alpergen—plus all her gear, including eduha pods."

The repair mech turned away, picked up the metal plate, and left the lounge. And a moment later, freed of her mentrol helmet and her control of the mech, Theodora Ellson rejoined me.

"I'll get their bags packed," she said.

Alpergen was struggling back toward awareness, groaning and muttering, and Grisa was conscious, but silent. I handed the needle gun to Theo.

"I'm dumping them both out the lock right now," I told her. "Maybe the ship will smell better then."

Theo smiled her appreciation as she swung the narrow-snouted weapon about in her competent small hand. I dragged Alpergen outside first, not caring too much when his body bumped into furnishings and bulkheads en route. And then I carried Grisa, kicking and screeching obscenely, after him and closed the outer locks.

"Now," Theo said, "I will pack their gear."

"And I'll help you," I said.

The ship *did* smell better, I realized, and I saw more clearly and heard better. It was as though a sodden curtain of smog had rolled back from my brain—a cloud that had smothered me for all the months Grisa had been my wife. I felt alive again despite the lingering numbness throughout my body.

There was one more little incident before the *Khan* blasted off for its touchdown on two-year distant Sebal. A passenger liner had suffered a blow-up when its main pile's controls malfunctioned, and its passengers had escaped to Kelso. In the years ensuing most of them had found transportation to their destination—distant Sebal! Only five of them, three men and two women, remained.

With my mate and my wife gone, I had room for five passengers and so they came aboard. One of their names sounded familiar. He was

150

a handsome, blond giant of a man, and very attentive to one of the middle-aged women of their party—the wealthy widow of a mine owner killed in the space disaster. His name was Blaiter.

So it was that I sent for Theo and they met in the chart room away from the rest of his party. I started to leave them but Theo grasped my sleeve. And Blaiter gasped as he saw who my mate was.

"Wait," she said, "this will be brief."

"Theo!" Blaiter gulped out. "How'd you get out here?"

"I came out to join you, Medson," she said, "on Sebal."

"But—I didn't … You didn't know anything about space. You couldn't sign on a ship."

"Oh that was simple." She laughed off-key and loudly. "I signed on as a utility hand. It wasn't bad; I learned a lot from the crew and the officers."

A series of expressions—disgust, anxiety, and sudden relief are what I ticketed them—flowed over his handsome fair features.

"Well," he said, and again, "well! That ends all thought of marriage of course. Why you're no better than a streetwalker, Theo! All those men …"

I started to say something, but Theo shook her head. "You mean you won't … even after you promised, Medson?" she demanded, her face hidden in her hands.

"I couldn't—even if I could forgive your actions. You see I was marooned here, penniless. So I married a wealthy woman—Mrs. Holson."

Theo's hands came away from her face and I was surprised to see that she was laughing. Then her features sobered. "In that case you can hand over the five thousand units, Medson. You won't be needing them for us."

Blaiter paled and started to protest. I watched him going through his pockets. His total assets were slightly over three thousand units. Then I took a hand.

"We need another utility hand aboard, Blaiter," I said. "I can sign you on, your wages to go to the mate."

"No—no! I'll get the money from Clara. Just wait a little while."

Blaiter turned and hurried away down the corridor. I took Theo's arm. "Why didn't you tell the truth about being aboard an alien ship like this—that the crew considers you as sexually desirable as an Earthman considers a female gorilla or chimp?"

Theo grinned impishly. "*You* forgot to mention that fact to me when I signed on, too, Captain. If I hadn't read somewhere about only Terran ships retaining that stupid section of the contract, I might have left ship in the asteroids. But I knew that you were chartered under Aantarian registry."

"You acted as though you believed me," I accused.

Theo laughed at my scowl. "Naturally," she said. "I wanted to know how far you might carry the bluff before I spoke."

"Women," I groaned weakly, and grinned. "What about Blaiter? Why did you lead him to believe such a thing?"

"Believe it or not," she said, "but I was cured the moment I saw him again. How else could I have driven him away so completely?"

I shook my head, admiring the dimple that came and went with her smile. How could I ever have thought her plain? Or perhaps it was something about space, and self confidence, and acquired poise that made her so attractive.

Blaiter came dashing in with the two thousand credits, tossed them at Theo, and vanished. The intercom came to life. It was approaching time for blast off with Sebal at the end of this hop. We headed for the control room together.

It was going to be a good tour ...

Final Voyage

Myra Lacey came swiftly down along the muddy ditch of trail that links the spaceport dump with the native city. Grayish ooze coated her plastic mudalls and had splashed as high as her shielded, pert-nosed face.

She clawed frantically at my outer lock. As she stumbled inside for the first time I sensed the vibrations of distant flameblasts and paralyzing *lectros*.

I knew what that meant. The threatened revolt of the Venusian colonists and their native "Frog" allies had broken out.

The girl's feet raced across the inner lock and I felt her hurrying down my empty, rusting corridors toward my galley. As she ran, she threw back the transparent hood designed to shield her wavy mop of bronze from the endless Venusian rain.

"Peter!" she called. "Volcano—Brand!"

An unlovely scrawny neck poked out through my open galley door and the gray-bearded old head capping it blinked watery gray eyes. Suddenly the huge black pipe projecting from the beard vomited smoke and ashes.

"Myra," he said sadly, "ain't I told you not to come busting in here without warning? Here I be wearing just my pants and undershirt. No way to greet the owner of the *Janelace*."

"Volcano!" gasped the girl. "The rebellion has come. They've taken over the city and the spaceport. The Earth garrison won't last a day."

"Nice going," applauded Volcano Manby, his loose-jointed old frame straightening painfully, "maybe now there'll be work enough to go around. About time Venus was free."

"But Volcano, they're mining the spaceport!" The girl was breathless. "Don't you understand? My brother Ralph's with the Earth fleet. Due here next week, all four ships. The rebels will mine the landing port—blow them up!"

"Myra!" The dark-eyed young man came up behind her with his quick hitching gait. Captain Peter Durfee had lost his leg in a power explosion just off Ganymede, an explosion that had cost him his ship and his job with Planetary Trading. Since then he had been living here in my old rusting hulk with two other unemployed spacers, Volcano and squatty Brand Parker.

"We've got to warn them, Peter." Myra's fingers clamped Durfee's arm nervously. "They've stripped all the space freighters in port of their fuel mixers; they can't take off. I thought maybe your radio beam could ..."

Durfee shook his head. His straight lips tightened. "I'm sorry, Myra," he said. "So far all my experiments have bumped into a blank wall. I can't punch through the Heaviside. Once in space the beam will carry messages for an unlimited distance, depending on the power of the impulse, but we are not in space."

"And won't be," said Myra bitterly. "If only the *Janelace* were in a shape for takeoff."

Volcano cleared his throat. "The old *Janelace*'d take off now," he said, "if we only had a goop mixer. We been working on the old tub these last three years, Myra, patching up the plates and trimming the jets. She'd carry us out into space easy."

"But we have no mixer." Durfee frowned and snapped his fingertips at a fraying cuff. "If the Frogs and the colonists have seized all the mixers, the *Janelace* is helpless."

"Couldn't we blast off with manual controls?" Myra demanded.

"And get the life jarred out of us with every blast even if the jets didn't explode?" Durfee shook his head. "Human bones will stand only so much. The rocket fuel must be fed into the jets in mathematically exact proportions at exact intervals—that's why we need that robot control."

"Nothing to worry about," a deep hoarse voice roared at Myra's elbow, and Brand Parker's squatty scarred body bowlegged past her to face the trio. "Nothing to worry about," he repeated with a blink of his one good eye.

"What do you mean, Brand?" Durfee snapped. "Not that I love the Earth fleet so much, but this trap the rebels are planning turns my stomach. When Earth learns of it they'll really bomb the life out of Venus. If we can prevent the fleet's destruction, Earth may grant us independence—"

"The *Janelace*'ll take off again," grinned Brand lopsidedly through his ragged pinkish moustache. "Yep, she'll take off again."

The thought of being in space again made me forget for the moment the conversation of the humans inside my clumsy bulk. A ship in the course of thirty or forty years of use in space absorbs the personalities and knowledge of her crews in a way that's hard to explain. Perhaps it's the action of the unshielded radiations out there in the blessed weightlessness of space, or perhaps …

So here I lay in the lowlands below the plateau island of Tular with the *thidin* vines covering my scaling plates and the ugly debris of Tular City's municipal dump heaped around me, and I was dreaming of the chill airlessness of space. I'd still be blasting out there, I reflected bitterly, if Planetary Trading hadn't planted one of their men on board to wreck my controls as we braked down for a landing here on Tular.

I'd been the last of Corwin Lacey's fleet of spacers to go, and when Corwin Lacey was killed in my final crash his daughter had found work as a waitress in one of Tular City's smelly cafes. With the stubborn pride of the Laceys, she and her brother had refused to sell my broken hulk for scrap. Someday they had hoped to repair my shattered drive mechanisms and again blast spaceward. Only two of the crew had stayed with me. Old Volcano Manby, the cook, and Brand Parker, a tube man. Later, they had brought a broken, drink-fogged wreck of a man to live with them in their quarters—the now trim-looking, graying-haired young captain without a ship, Peter Durfee.

And for three long years I'd wallowed in the sour smell of gray Venusian mudland with the scaly yellow *vallids* scrabbling lizard-like across my plates and nesting in my rocket tubes, while the *nik-nik* brush and snaky twining thidin vines closed in to bury me from the sight of men …

"Brand, you dirty pirate!" Captain Durfee's voice was suddenly more alive and vibrant with excitement than I had ever heard it before. "Not that I blame you for not reporting your discovery of that missing Planetary freighter before, but—ten crated mixers!"

"Wouldn't have got more than fifty credits reward for finding them," grumbled Brand. "No more than fifty. Nope. Wouldn't buy another mixer for the *Janelace*."

"This may save Ralph's neck, and block a real war with Earth, Myra!" Durfee's arm was tight around the girl's waist, and she seemed pleased that it was there. I may be a welded conglomeration of metal and plastics, but I know what love means. They were just finding out.

Volcano grumbled. His pipe had gone out, and he was ladling a new charge of homegrown greenish tobacco into its amazingly capacious maw.

"A goop mixer weighs quarter of a ton," he pointed out. "You said the wreck's three miles out in the swamp. How do we get one of them here? Fly it out? Or hire a half dozen swamp Frogs to freight it out on their backs?"

"We'll use mud boats." Captain Durfee's voice was crisp and incisive. "Today we'll check over the ship and get it ready for space. I imagine the vallids have fouled up the jets again with their nests; they'll have to be cleaned out. Check up on the two spacesuits, Brand, we may need them if the *Janelace* cracks open on the takeoff."

"Do I smell something burning?" Myra wrinkled her generous uptilted nose.

"My stew!" Volcano dashed madly into the galley.

"You boys haven't eaten yet?" Myra smiled. "Of course not. I came back from the city when I first heard the news. The boss will be firing me if I don't hurry back."

"He'll never miss you." Durfee laughed. "There'll be so much excitement in Tular City today that there'll be no eating. Better stick around for lunch."

"What you having, Volcano?" Myra called.

"Vallid steaks and stew," Volcano admitted gloomily.

"With thidin shoots and nik-nik fruit on the side," groaned Durfee. "That's our regular diet here aboard the *Janelace*. If it wasn't for the stale bread and cakes Brand wangles from the wife of some city baker we'd get indigestion."

"Why, Brand!" Myra grinned cheerfully at the tube man's reddening face. "I'm learning a lot about you today."

She turned to Durfee. "Sorry, Peter," she said sweetly, "but I think I'll eat at the cafe today. I'll get enough swamp food after we blast off for Earth."

With a squeeze of Durfee's arm she was gone back along my corridor. She adjusted the transparent hood of her mudalls as she opened my outer lock and went out into the misty thickness of the outer atmosphere.

"She thinks we'll take her along!" Durfee rubbed at his bleached-out square chin. "But she can't go. I doubt if we have fuel enough to more than escape Venus' drag. There'll be no landing on Earth or any other planet."

"One way trip?" Brand scratched at his scraggly pink locks with a thick-nailed thumb. "Oh well, suits me fine, just fine. Be good to see the stars again. Stars and sun. Good place to die. Yep, good place."

Volcano's pipe jutted around the doorframe. Smoke belched. "Ain't you spacers hungry?" he demanded. "Fill up. We got plenty work to do."

"Leave the dishes, Volcano." Durfee was strapping on one of his ancient revolvers, one of the dozens salvaged from the tons of debris heaped around my resting place. "We're going out to take a look at the wreck."

"Follow my directions carefully," warned Brand. "In this everlasting fog you can lose your way easily. Lose it very easily. Maybe I better go along. Maybe I better."

"You have work enough here checking the tubes and the wiring," said Captain Durfee as he zippered shut the front of his patched yellowish mudalls. "If you get all the vallid nests dug out before we get back, you can gather thidin shoots, mush roots, and shoot a few more vallids."

"Yessir," said Brand. Now that an emergency had come the old easy relationship was gone. Durfee was the captain now.

Volcano struggled and wriggled his lanky warped old body into another of the yellowed plastic envelopes that are standard equipment for mudland colonists on Venus and with his unlit pipe clenched between his teeth followed Durfee out of the galley. I saw them go down to the vine-hidden dock where their two flat-bottomed swamp boats were tied, and then the swirling grayish mist swallowed them.

Deep down inside my vitals, Brand worked with wrenches and blowtorch. He checked over the crude but sturdy repairs they had made upon my twisted plates and framework. He tested the circuits that operated the emergency locks and the individual fire controls of each of my sixty-seven major and minor jets. And on the swivel joints of the dozens of hydroponic tanks, where the oxygen-freeing green growths of three worlds luxuriated, he squirted oil.

Then he went outside to check my jets. The wooden plugs that sealed off their narrow mouths were covered with fungus and purple mould, so he did not touch them; but half a dozen of my main jets had been invaded by the lizard-like vallids and these he set about ejecting from their snug nests. Brand knew that any obstruction, even the eggs or bony-plated body of a vallid, might cause the rocket tubes to explode. The jets must be cleared of all foreign matter.

Brand grinned suddenly, his scarred face twisting. "They hate smoke," he chuckled to himself, "especially tobacco smoke. Yep, tobacco smoke. Remember when Volcano drove off half a dozen of 'em with that pipe of his."

A quick trip back into his quarters yielded about four pounds of the flaky green-leaved tobacco that Volcano smoked. This he divided into six piles and heaped deep inside the tubes. A moment later six trickles of acrid smoke rolled sluggishly out into the shifting dank fog.

The tube man scurried for the shelter of my outer lock—nor was he a moment too soon. For from the jet's interiors vallids came boiling out, great five-foot lengths of black-splotched yellowish ferocity with snaggle-toothed long snouts gaping savagely. Behind the males came the shorter-snouted females, their eight stubby legs clawing them along, and their jaws champing angrily as they kept up an eternal complaining whistle.

Most of the vallids headed for the swamplands at once but two of the more persistent required a touch or two of Brand's flameblast before they retreated. After that it was a simple matter to rake out the empty nests, and the few lopsided reddish eggs in two of them, before turning an air hose into the jets.

Brand plugged the cleaned jets before he left, and spent the remainder of the day polishing up my corroded control-room metal. From time to time he peered out the porthole facing the landing dock, and by chance saw the return of Durfee and Volcano Manby.

They were not alone. Five of the short, gray-skinned Frogs, the naked web-footed natives of the Venusian swamplands, were with them, and balanced on a framework linking the two mud boats sat the crated cube that was a fuel mixer!

He hurried down the soupy slope to join them as they brought the boats ashore. With the help of the natives the mixer was on the semi-solid mud of the landing before he reached them.

"We'll be blasting off in the morning," said Durfee tautly.

"How about the natives?" Brand asked, frowning. "Won't they report our having a goop mixer? Won't they?"

"These are swampers." Durfee barked something at the Venusians in their native tongue and they heaved up on the poles lashed across the mixer's bulk. "They don't know there's been a revolt yet. By the time they do report us we'll be gone—or dead!"

The five Venusians and the three Earthmen staggered up the sticky slope, their feet sinking deep into the quaggy gray soil. Once they reached the cargo lock, however, Durfee ordered the mixer set down.

"Go get your tobacco, Volcano," ordered Captain Durfee. "About a pound for each man. And give them five of those necklaces you've been making of plastic bottle tops."

"Lucky I had another four pounds of tobacco stored away," said Volcano half an hour later as they eased the mixer down upon its permanent mountings in the engine room. "Those Frogs cleaned out the rest of it."

Brand chuckled, choked and then snorted loudly again. "You'll be sucking a dry pipe this flight, Volcano," he said. "I used that extra tobacco you had hidden to smoke out the vallids."

Volcano lunged at the squatty spaceman, his long legs tripping over the rollers they had used in transporting the mixer from the cargo lock. He sprawled into Brand, knocking him down, too. They rolled over and over on the deck, the waterproof strips of the mixer's protective envelope tangling around them stickily. Brand's fists thudded meatily into Volcano's skinny ribs, and the lanky cook's sharp elbows jabbed savagely into Brand's sides and face.

Durfee reached down and jerked the two men apart. He grinned boyishly, his face shedding for the moment the dour lines gained in the preceding gloomy four years.

"Won't you ever grow up?" he demanded. "Go out and get some nik-nik leaves, Volcano. You used to smoke them before you started growing your own tobacco."

Volcano growled something under his breath and headed for the galley.

"Let's get this mixer hooked up tonight, Brand," said Durfee, "so if we have to blast off in the forenoon, after Myra leaves for work, we'll be ready to go.

"Only," he paused and his dark eyes were pained, "don't tell her we're ready to leave. Let her think she's going with us."

But with the steaming morning light of the hidden sun I knew that Myra was destined to go with us on our mad flight into outer space. For, from the mile-distant barrier that surrounded the spaceport, a column of armed Frogs and revolting colonists was marching raggedly toward us.

I tried to warn Volcano as he worked over his stove in the galley, but the creaking of a slightly loosened girder and the rattle of an electrical cable beneath my deck could carry no message to the lanky old cook's hairy ears.

He was grumbling as he sucked at his empty pipe, and when he put down a dish he landed it with an emphatic slam. And the party of rebellious Venusians was slogging steadily nearer.

Captain Peter Durfee was working over a chart in the navigation blister. A filing cabinet was bolted to the deck behind him and I fought the worn bolt that secured its left corner. Suddenly the metal parted and Durfee's head snapped up with the sound. His eyes glanced momentarily outside, as I had hoped they would, and he saw the shadowy outlines of the approaching force.

He snapped over the worn switch of the intercommunication system and pressed the little red stud in its side. The staccato buzz of the general alarm echoed through the metal hollowness of my four hundred feet of rusting metal—the signal to prepare to abandon ship, or prepare for crash landing.

"Brand!" he barked into the mouthpiece. "We've got to unplug the main jets. Don't bother with the auxils; we can remove them in space if the cold doesn't shrink them enough to drop out. I'll take care of the braking jets in the bow.

"Volcano!" He waited for the cook's reply. "There's a party of Venusians coining. Get one of the converted gas rifles and cover me when I try to free the braking jets. Don't shoot to kill; we're on their side only they don't know it."

Under his breath Durfee cursed as he snapped off the switch. If only he had insisted that Myra Lacey get a room in Tular City, rather than keep on living aboard …

He slipped into his plastic mud gear and ran out of my forward lock, a hammer and short pointed bar in his hands. Quickly he drove the bar into one of my sealed tubes with a rap of the hammer and jerked at the plug. With a plop the plug came free, and he hurried on to my next braking jet.

Ten of the twelve jets in my blunt bow were free when the Venusians came within range. They came forward then at the double, their flameblasts breathing searing yellow jets, and their paralyzing lectros snapping and crackling as their invisible bolts of energy lashed out at Durfee. Pale nik-nik brush and the pulpy purple-veined vines of thidin blackened and withered all around Durfee but the young spacer doggedly worked away at his task of clearing the jets.

The cough of a gas gun, one of the ancient rifles equipped with a pressure tank of rocket fuel instead of utilizing water-hungry gunpowder, sounded then, and sudden bursts of explosive bullets threw up jets of mud in the attackers' faces. They hugged the ground, slithering quickly into the water-filled depressions that would afford some measure of protection. Old Volcano Manby was in action at last.

Durfee cleared the last two jets quickly, and jumping down from the half-rotten scaffolding of poles that reached almost to my forward control blister, he raced back toward the main driving jets. From there had come the fog-muffled sounds of battle.

A party of Frogs had circled down along the swamp and come by boat to take Brand by surprise from the rear. The jets were clear, but Brand crouched behind a spongy fallen log while the Frogs poured a barrage of flame at his shelter. Steam poured upward, but as yet Brand was untouched.

Captain Durfee shouted as he rounded the blunt swell of my side, tugging at the rebuilt old revolver, also gas-operated, in his waterproof holster. The Frogs lost all stomach for battle as he poured explosive bullets in their general direction, and they headed back toward the swamp.

"Let's go, Brand!" shouted Durfee, yanking at the dazed oldster's shoulder.

Brand weaved to his feet, sweat pouring down his face and soaking his ragged pink moustache. He blinked his one good eye. Steam was yet pouring from his patched mudalls.

"Broiled like a lobster," he whispered hoarsely. "Broiled alive."

Durfee fed a warming blast into my jets. I felt new life quiver through my ancient frame, and I sensed the insidious tug of the swamp mud at my lower plates. Volcano climbed down from the upper blister where he had been holding off the attackers and hurried into my galley. There were loose dishes to be battened down before the takeoff. And Myra Lacey strapped herself into one of the worn pressure seats in my control room ready for the initial shock of the blast off.

"First pancakes in two months," grumbled Volcano, champing savagely at his lifeless pipe, "and we can't eat 'em."

"I hope that number five doesn't blow," muttered Brand uneasily as he checked the gauges deep down in my vitals, "we patched her up as best we could but ..."

"Ready, darling?" asked Durfee as he sent another, hotter, blast roaring out into the sticky dankness of the mudlands.

"Any time," smiled Myra. She bit her lip. "Blast off," she said, "any time you're ready, Peter."

"Volcano—Brand," Durfee said crisply into the intercom mouthpiece, "blasting off."

His hand tugged downward gently on the controls that linked with the mixer. The blasting of my jets deepened and steadied. I quivered and fought back at the hungry fingers of the swamp. The slimy mud slipped suddenly from my rusty old plates and the rotted scaffolding at my bow crumpled as I surged skyward at an almost horizontal angle.

Steering jets thundered at Durfee's trained touch. I curved upward more steeply, the endless clouds of Venus smothering all vision of what lay behind us. I felt a main drive tube explode, but I bored onward. I was empty, my cargo bins hollow and my fuel tanks less than a third full. When I was younger three jets could have carried me beyond the tug of Venusian gravity.

"We'll chart a course about Venus," Durfee was saying breathlessly, "that will make the *Janelace* a satellite. Then when the Earth fleet comes within range of my radio beam we can warn them."

He smiled rather grimly at Myra. "That's providing the *Janelace* holds together long enough to reach such an orbit," he added.

And at that moment, as the secondary cloud envelope of Venus thinned and the sun shone through, I felt my plates grinding and my inner girders twisting. The stress of the blast off, and now the sudden decrease in the outer atmospheric pressure on my weakened structure, was too much for me. Great sections of my skin ripped free. Air hissed out through a thousand rents, and automatic doors clanged shut. Alarm lights blinked. Buzzers went mad.

The control room was intact, and down in the tube room Brand was clamping shut the helmet of one of the two spacesuits hanging there. He yelped through the intercom that he was all right.

"How about you, Volcano?" Durfee asked.

He heard a connected string of warmly purple space oaths. "I'll be okay," he roared, "if these pancakes hold out."

"Pancakes!" gasped Captain Durfee blankly.

"Yep." The sound of teeth grinding on a pipestem was plainly audible. "I'm plastering them on the leaks. They freeze fast as the air pressure squeezes 'em through."

Durfee laughed. "Once we hit our orbit we'll rig up some low pressure patches and link the galley and the control room together. Until then keep the pancakes working."

"Yes, sir!" agreed Volcano emphatically. "I will!"

A matter of twenty-four hours later a cruiser out near Lunar, pirate-patrolling, answered Captain Durfee's beamed radio call, and a rescue ship, a freighter, headed in our direction. The warning of the Venusian rebels' trap was relayed to Earth by means of a speedy two-man jetter. And word was flashed back along Durfee's beam that the World Union had granted Venus autonomy only three days before! Their rebellion had been needless!

The unshielded sun of space felt good on my old plates. There was no relentless drag of gravity here to warp and strain my weary framework. Drowsily I heard Captain Durfee and Myra, talking with their heads very close together.

"The beam will make you wealthy," Myra was saying. "You can buy another freighter and we'll recommission the *Janelace*. We'll show Planetary Trading we're a long way from being licked."

Durfee shook his head. His arm tightened around Myra. "No, dear," he said. "The *Janelace* has made her last voyage. We're going to hook a solar reflector on her and leave her here to circle Venus eternally. She's earned that.

"We'll come out to visit her occasionally, and we'll tell our grandchildren how she averted war between Earth and Venus."

Down in the galley Brand laughed and slapped a stubby-fingered hand against his bowlegs. Volcano snarled, his pipe bobbling angrily. The smell of the nik-nik leaves made both their eyes water.

"A filthy habit," said Brand soberly, waggling his head. "A filthy habit." He pawed savagely at his pink moustache, and his eyes leaked moisture …

The sun, shielded from me so long by the cloud-shell of Venus, felt good on my old plates. The chill of space crept in and the sunlight routed it as I slowly revolved. I dreamed of the voyages I had made in those dimming years. Long forgotten faces of the crews that had lived, and fought, and worked between my decks grew more vivid as I drifted there, inert and weightless.

Space had claimed me at last.

Checklist of Sources

Note: The checklist below gives the original publication source for each of the stories included in this collection.

Under Martian Sands
Out of This World Adventures, December 1950

Monster No More
Orbit Science Fiction, Vol. 1, No. 1, 1953

Ship of the Fog Seas
Spaceway Science Fiction, April 1955

Stalemate
Worlds of If Science Fiction, November 1954

The Pioneers
Worlds of If Science Fiction, June 1955

Memorium
Fantastic Universe, March 1956

Second Sight
Fantastic Universe, September 1957

Sole Survivor
Satellite Science Fiction, December 1957

Moment of Truth
Fantastic Universe, December 1957

Utility Girl
The Original Science Fiction Stories, May 1959

Final Voyage
Science Fiction Adventures, *December 1957*